ALL
I HAVE
IS BLUE

Also by James Colbert

PROFIT AND SHEEN
NO SPECIAL HURRY
SKINNY MAN

ALL
I HAVE
IS BLUE

James Colbert

ATHENEUM • NEW YORK • 1992

Maxwell Macmillan Canada • Toronto

Maxwell Macmillan International
New York • Oxford • Singapore • Sydney

Copyright © 1992 by James Colbert

Atheneum   Maxwell Macmillan Canada, Inc.
Macmillan Publishing Company   200 Eglinton Avenue East
866 Third Avenue   Suite 200
New York, NY 10022   Don Mills, Ontario M3C 3N1

Macmillan Publishing Company is part of the Maxwell Communication Group of Companies.

Library of Congress Cataloging-in-Publication Data
Colbert, James.
    All I have is blue / James Colbert.
      p.   cm.
    ISBN 0-689-12157-1
    I. Title.
    PS3553.04385A6   1992
      813'.54—dc20   91-35150   CIP

10 9 8 7 6 5 4 3 2 1

Printed in the United States of America

FOR DAVID HECHLER
with respect, with admiration,
with thanks

ALL
I HAVE
IS BLUE

1

The black, unblinking eyes were fixed on his face. The black, diamond-shaped head was raised slightly, above the snake's coiled body, alert and poised. Bent over awkwardly, his long, stalklike legs placed apart for stability, both hands grasping one end of the driftwood log he had just begun to lift, Skinny froze; and he stayed like that, unmoving, not knowing what else to do—not with the snake less than six feet away on the other end of the log. Behind him, he heard Ruth giving a running account of the things she was finding.

Skinny and Ruth were on the batture of the Mississippi River, in the area between the levee and the river itself. They were just below Catfish Bend, across a half mile of deceptively placid water from Sugar House Point, fifteen miles downriver from downtown New Orleans. The air was cool, but the bright sun was warm. The sky was high and blue overhead.

"And over here," Ruth said, poking around in the weeds, "another find for Skinny: another old tire! Better put it with the others."

"Jesus Christ," Skinny said to himself, perturbed by his predicament but blaming it mostly on himself.

Three weeks before, Skinny had suggested in passing to Ruth that she clean up her patio, which, unexpectedly, she had. Then she had decided to decorate the newly clean space with pieces of driftwood. This Sunday had been unseasonably warm, and Skinny had not been quick enough to come up with an excuse to avoid helping Ruth find the driftwood she wanted. So they had taken his truck and together they had been exploring the big bend in the river. Once he had begun looking around, Skinny had been amazed by the things that had washed up on the batture: so far he had found household furniture and appliances, three tires in reasonably good condition, even a nearly full gallon of thirty-weight oil. He had, in fact, found a variety of flotsam that included just about everything *but* driftwood, an omission he had only begun to rectify when he had found the snake.

He tensed his back, ready to heave the log—and the big water moccasin coiled on top of the other end of it—to one side. Then he heard Ruth nearby, and he relaxed slightly, holding off, not wanting the snake to go in her direction, getting more aggravated by the second.

Skinny had been a policeman for eleven years. After a brief go at college, he had gone to work for the New Orleans Police Department, and in that time he had been shot at, kicked, bitten, assaulted with a whole assortment of weapons and instruments; but this was, without doubt, the first time he had ever been stuck with his butt up in the air.

Suddenly, a long stick, an old, bent branch, moved beside him, moving forward. The tip of the stick poked the snake in one fat coil, then pushed it off the log. Skinny jumped back as the snake fell, flipped around convulsively, and slowly slithered away.

Beside him, Ruth said, "I couldn't understand why you were just standing there like that. You didn't look very comfortable."

Ruth was almost as tall as Skinny, and almost as angular. Her red-blond hair was puffed out, sort of parted high on one side. Her face was long, finished with too square a jaw, but when she was smiling, as she was just then, obviously pleased that she had come to the rescue, the evident good humor outshone her too-square features.

"Skinny *wasn't* very comfortable," Skinny admitted, referring to himself as he almost always did, as if to another person, watching as the snake disappeared into a patch of knee-high grass.

"The weather has been cold," Ruth added. "Probably it wasn't even awake."

"It was awake enough for me," Skinny said, relieved that the snake was gone, noting the way Ruth minimized her assistance. In the five months he had known her, Skinny had come to like Ruth a lot. He liked her quick-witted humor and the constancy of her outlook, optimistic and realistic at the same time. He liked her confident, uncomplaining self-sufficiency. There was something solid about her. He had learned to rely on her judgment, and he had even learned to deal with the fact that she was usually a half step ahead of him—though as often as possible he liked to play that against her.

"So now that you've saved my life," he predicted, "you think I should find some driftwood, right?"

"Right," Ruth affirmed readily. She used her long stick to point at one of the items nearby that Skinny had uncovered earlier, a rusted and waterlogged full-sized appliance. "Ruth already has a dishwasher, thank you."

"You do?" Skinny asked, stopping to think, curious because he had never seen her use it.

Ruth glanced at him out of the corners of her eyes.

"As long as you're around, I do," she laughed, and playfully she held the stick up high and dipped it toward him, pretending to whack him on the head.

Skinny made a grab for the stick, but Ruth pulled it out of reach. He moved toward her. Ruth backed up, feigning a wide-eyed fear, and held the stick low, like a lance; but their game was interrupted when a horn blasted deafeningly. The sound was a vibrating presence that startled them both, and they both spun around to see what it was.

Not a hundred yards away, an offshore supply boat was running in close to shore, coming around the turn in the river, its powerful diesel engines rumbling. The boat was all metal, small but very obviously seaworthy. It was painted dark green. On the bow, a young boy was bent over, securing something to the deck. In the pilot house, a man was leaning out the window, laughing and shaking his finger at them waggishly. When Ruth waved back, swinging her stick back and forth like a flag, the man tooted the boat's horn twice in a friendly greeting and increased the throttle. The boat surged past, white water churning in its wake.

"Saved by the horn," Ruth said, and quickly jumped away, picking up where they had left off.

"Ha," Skinny said, starting after her, but just then, out on the water, there was a powerful, muffled thump that stopped them again.

Ruth glanced at Skinny, but Skinny was looking downriver, seeing that the supply boat that had just passed them was now, apparently, dead in the water. The stern of the boat was drifting out lazily toward midriver, already caught in the current. Sunlight reflected on the pilot house windows, and as Skinny raised his hand to shield his eyes from the glare, there was a second heavy thump, more powerful than the first.

The pilot house windows exploded outward.

The rear deck buckled, and the boat immediately went down on the stern, pitched forward, then rocked back again, its green hull settling low in the dirty, brown water.

"Jesus Christ," Skinny said, his voice loud and nasal.

Ruth started to ask what had happened, but Skinny had already turned and was moving away from her, quick-stepping his naturally overlong strides, flapping his arms, elbows high as he hurried across the batture and up the levee to his truck.

Ruth set out behind him but picked her way more cautiously.

From the top of the levee, Skinny could see heavy smoke billowing out from the pilot house and water boiling around the stern of the boat. On the bow, he saw the young boy sprawled across the deck, his head between his arms, rigidly clutching a cleat.

He started his truck, backed down the levee, waited for Ruth to jump in.

"What happened?" she asked. She had to use both hands to pull shut the door.

"The boat blew up," Skinny replied, irritably stating the obvious.

The truck's tires spun before they took hold.

Skinny glanced at Ruth apologetically.

"Hold on," he said, and he drove up the levee then down the top of it, heading downstream. The packed dirt was uneven, and the ground moved past in a rough, jarring blur. The driftwood Ruth had put in the back of the truck bounced and slid, thumping heavily against the bed.

"My God, Skinny," Ruth said, looking out at the river. "That little boy is still on the boat."

Skinny acknowledged that with a dour nod.

"Skinny should've stayed home and watched the football game on TV." He glanced at the boat. "So should've he—that boat won't be afloat much longer."

"There are other people on board, Skinny. The man in the pilot house—"

"He should've stayed home, too."

Skinny was trying to keep the truck on the road and at the same time he was trying to calculate how far downriver the boat would drift as he swam out to it. He knew that the river was very fast and unforgiving, filled with the flotsam he had before found so intriguing, but he didn't see any way around it. He had to get wet.

"This is *not* how I had planned to spend my day off," Skinny noted for the record.

Ruth smiled wanly, but her eyes remained fixed, looking past him.

A full quarter mile past the boat, Skinny stopped and jumped out of the truck, unzipping his sleeveless green fatigue jacket as he did so, taking it off and throwing it into the back of the truck.

"Try to keep me in sight," Skinny said as he bent over to unlace his boots. He stripped off his jeans and put his boots back on. "Move the truck down as the boat drifts." He pulled the boot laces tight and knotted them. "If a car goes past"—he waved at the river road on the far side of the levee—"try to stop it. Tell whoever is driving to call the coast guard."

Ruth nodded and slid across the seat of the truck, moving behind the wheel. Skinny started to turn away, but she stopped him.

"Skinny," she said, looking right at him and waiting for him to look back. When he did, she said very sternly, "You be careful."

Skinny made a sour face.

"Jesus Christ in a wheelbarrow," he remarked, and started on down the levee.

Ruth shut the door of the truck and watched Skinny through the window. Wearing only his baggy boxer shorts and his green, canvas-topped boots, taking his humorously overlong strides, flapping his elbows for balance as he moved, he looked for all the world like a snowy egret in a hurry. Ruth smiled to herself, then glanced quickly up and down the river road, trying not to worry, trying to reassure herself that help would come along. When no cars appeared, she glanced back toward the river and saw that Skinny was already at the water's edge. Unhesitatingly, he went on in; he went out waist-deep before he dove forward and began to swim.

2

The water was colder than Skinny had expected, and the current was more powerful, a relentless, pushing force, a pressing weight. Keeping his boots on, he quickly realized, had not been such a great idea; but he had knotted them so tightly, he wasn't able to get them off.

"Brilliant," he chided himself, not in his best possible humor.

When he had first begun to swim, Skinny had been able to smell the water, the silt and the chemicals in it, but now his arms were tired and his legs were tired and he was just treading water, considerably more concerned with what he could see than with what he could smell: the supply boat was drifting toward him too fast, dangerously fast. A few moments before, he had seen a big balloon of air escape to the surface, and the boat had gone down even farther on the stern. He knew he had to let the boat go past, then approach it from behind, avoiding the turbulence and whatever was causing it—avoiding the boat itself, which with its weight alone could very easily run right over him.

He glanced at the shore, looking for his truck, and saw Ruth looking back at him, dutifully keeping abreast.

"I *should* be on my couch right now," he said to her, knowing full well that she could not possibly hear him. "I *should* be watching the game, eating a few chips, waiting for my pizza." He started to wave, to let her know that he was okay, but at the last possible moment he saw a dark shadow beneath the surface, a tree or a log, it was hard to tell which, bearing right down on him.

"Jesus Christ," he said, kicking away from it, feeling the soft, water-soaked branches scrape his legs, feeling them moving, waving in the current like the grasping arms of some great, living creature.

Skinny gave the tree a wide berth, and by the time it had passed, the boat was nearly on top of him, close enough that he could see each rivet in its heavy steel hull and the orange rust on the seams. He swam astern of it then up onto the rear deck that slanted right down to the water to meet him.

The deck plates had been torn and twisted, blown outward around the edge of a jagged hole at least six feet across. The brown river water was flowing into and out of the hole, lapping against the buckled plates around it, and even as Skinny pulled himself up onto the deck, he felt his weight displace more air from the hull. He saw big bubbles coming up from somewhere beneath the surface.

"This baby is going down," he noted grimly as he worked his way forward, crawling, one hand on the raised gunwale, trying at first to see past the smoke from the pilot house, then as he got near it, looking into the pilot house itself. Directly beneath the ship's wheel, there was another jagged hole in the deck, and across from it, crumpled against the far bulkhead, there was a man's battered and broken body.

Skinny got to his feet, and, bent low, avoiding the hole in the deck, he stepped into the pilot house and squatted down next to the man, waving away the smoke, trying to see. Quickly, he rolled the man onto his back and pressed his ear against his chest, confirming what was already apparent: the man was dead.

Skinny rocked back on his heels and for a long moment just looked at him, making sure that he would be able to describe him, momentarily thinking of the impulse that had prompted the man to blow the boat's horn at Ruth and him.

The man was black, of medium build, with a broad flat nose and strangely shaped ears that seemed too small for his head. Blood had dribbled from the corner of his mouth, dark red against his dark, purple-black skin. Both his legs were gone, blown off above his knees.

He must have been standing right there, Skinny thought, quickly glancing back at the ship's wheel and the jagged hole beneath it, *there where we saw him*.

Smoke was swirling through the pilot house, coming up from below deck, but for a few seconds it changed direction and blew toward the front of the boat. In those few seconds, Skinny tried to go forward to look below deck, but a tongue of orange-yellow flame flared up suddenly, driving him back.

The smoke shifted again, and Skinny noticed two things: a life jacket near the door and an unusual pistol lying next to it, a kind he had never before seen. He picked them both up and quickly went back outside, away from the smoke, just glancing at the pistol before he tossed it away, seeing no reason to try to swim carrying it, into the water that now completely covered the hole in the deck. He started forward again, toward the bow.

The boy was just where he had been since Skinny had

first seen him, but he had changed position: now he was sitting up, his hands beside his hips, clutching the ends of the cleat. He was younger than Skinny had thought, only ten or eleven years old, and he had the same small, strangely shaped ears as the man Skinny had found in the pilot house. The boy's black hair was cut short. His black eyes darted back and forth, wide with fear.

"This is Skinny," Skinny said, and thumped a finger against his own chest. "Who are you?"

After a moment, the boy replied, "Dwayne," sullenly.

"Dwayne," Skinny asked, "is there anyone else on the boat? Other than you"—he gestured back at the pilot house—"and the man in there?"

The boy shook his head no.

"Just me and my father."

Damn, Skinny said to himself. He ran both hands through his wet hair, then hitched up his shorts, deciding to try to get the boy off the boat before he told him about his father. "So, Dwayne," he said, "you ready to take a swim?" When the boy did not reply, he moved closer, avoiding a big coil of rope on the deck, and added, "When I was your age, I used to swim in the river for fun—I nearly drowned my ass once and gave it up." He took another step forward. "Put this on," he ordered, and held out the sun-faded orange life jacket.

The boy did not take the jacket but stared past Skinny at the pilot house, his eyes uncertain and fearful.

"What about my father?" he asked.

Skinny stepped near the boy and squatted down so that he was looking up at him, seeing the flawless brown skin on his cheeks and his small, strangely shaped ears. He pressed his lips together tightly until he figured out what to say next.

"Dwayne, we can't help your father, partner," he said

finally. "He's dead. Something blew up right where he was standing."

The boy blinked once, then blinked again, his eyes no longer fearful but hurt and uncomprehending.

Skinny draped the life jacket over Dwayne's shoulders and guided one of his arms through it.

Dwayne reluctantly put his other arm through himself.

"Can't just leave him here," he said quietly as Skinny tied the straps on the chest.

"We have to," Skinny replied.

Skinny picked up Dwayne as he stood up. Holding him chest-high, he went to the railing and stepped over it, pausing just a moment to check the water. He felt the boat tremble ominously, and he saw Dwayne hide his face in his chest. He waved at Ruth, signaling that he was bringing the boy to shore.

3

The boat stayed afloat only long enough for Skinny and Dwayne to get well away from it. In the water, Skinny sidestroked alongside Dwayne, pulling him toward shore by a strap on the life jacket, and they both watched as it got lower and lower, going down stern-first, until it slipped beneath the surface, leaving behind only a small slick of oil.

"You doing all right?" Skinny asked, hoping to get Dwayne to look away from the spot where the boat had gone down, but Dwayne did not seem to hear him. After that, Skinny was quiet, uncertain what else to say. He could remember very clearly when he had been Dwayne's age, about fifth grade, he figured, and he could imagine how he would have felt if at that age he had seen his own father killed. So he put off the questions he wanted to ask and just swam, pulling hard against the powerful current, keeping an eye out for flotsam.

Where Skinny and Dwayne came out of the water was over two miles downriver from where Skinny had gone in. Skinny carried Dwayne until the water was only knee-deep, then he set him down and Dwayne walked.

Ruth was right there with the truck.

Once they were on solid ground, Ruth knelt next to Dwayne to help him off with the life jacket, and she saw that he was already starting to shiver.

"Into the truck with you," she said, and patted him on the rear. "The heater's on."

Skinny took his jacket from the back of the truck, wadded it up, and used it like a towel, quickly wiping himself down, starting to shiver himself. He shook out the jacket and put it on, then before he closed it, vigorously rubbed his chest.

"Skinny had almost forgotten he had nipples," he said when he saw Ruth watching him. "But they're there, all right." After a moment, he stopped his rubbing and tried to get the jacket's zipper to zip.

"Let me," Ruth offered, and moved in front of him, adding as she took charge of the zipper, "No cars came by. Not one."

Skinny acknowledged that with a nod.

"We have to find a phone."

Ruth got the zipper to work, then glanced into the truck as Skinny stepped around her to get his jeans.

"What about—?" she began. She lowered her voice. "Were there any others?"

"Just the man we saw at the wheel," Skinny replied. "He was dead." He looked directly at Ruth. "He was the boy's father."

"My God," she said softly. She glanced into the truck and saw Dwayne sitting in the middle of the seat, shoulders hunched forward, chin on his chest. "Skinny," she said, looking back, "you did great."

Skinny had put one foot up on the rear tire and was trying to unknot the lace in his boot. He looked up and started to say something to that, but Ruth had already opened the door and was getting into the truck.

Dwayne sat between Ruth and Skinny, his eyes dull and empty, as Skinny drove straight up the levee then down the other side of it. He turned onto the river road and went back upstream, toward New Orleans. Ruth put her arm around Dwayne and held him close to her side.

A few miles away, there was a restaurant in an old house, and near it, in the gravel parking lot, there was a pay phone on a pole. Skinny pulled in next to the phone and put the truck out of gear.

"Dwayne," he said, "listen, partner. Skinny has to report what happened, and he has to ask you a few questions, okay?"

The boy nodded.

Ruth rubbed his arm reassuringly.

"What was your father's name?" Skinny asked.

"Evans," the boy replied. "Evans Charles."

"Is that your last name, too? Charles?"

Dwayne nodded again.

"What was the name of the boat?"

"Boat didn't have no name."

"Did it have a number?"

Dwayne shrugged.

"Where were you going?" Ruth asked, leaning forward slightly so she could look at Dwayne as she spoke to him.

"My daddy didn't tell me," Dwayne replied, "just said I could come along, just me and him."

"Had you gone with your father before?"

"Once." Dwayne held his legs out straight and tapped the toes of his high-topped sneakers together.

"How long were you gone the last time?"

Dwayne shrugged.

"Were you gone overnight?"

He nodded.

"Longer?"

He nodded again.

"How much longer? Where did you go?"

"Went down someplace people didn't speak English—couldn't understand what they said."

Ruth glanced up, looking pointedly—disapprovingly—over Dwayne's head at Skinny, then she looked down again, her features softening.

"You went that far in that little boat?"

Dwayne nodded.

"What did your mother say?"

"Ain't got no momma. She gone."

"Where did she go?"

Dwayne shrugged.

"Just went off—when I was little."

"Who do you stay with when your father's gone?" Skinny asked. "When he makes trips and you don't go with him?"

"Stay with my auntee."

"Where does she live?"

"Over by the Silver Lily Club—that where she works. Got a house look out on the river."

"Does she have a phone?"

Dwayne shook his head.

"What's her name?"

"Agnes. She work during the day, don't come home 'til the evenings."

"So she's at the Silver Lily Club now?"

Dwayne shook his head again.

"She at church now or out visiting her friends. It Sunday."

Dwayne shoved his hands deep in his pockets and sank down on the seat, obviously tired of answering questions.

Skinny had all that he needed to make a report, so he leaned forward and looked for quarters in the tray that sat on top of the hump over the transmission. When he had three or four, he rubbed his hands on his arms with a quick friction-warming motion, then got out to use the phone.

Skinny found the listing for the Silver Lily Club and left a message for Agnes before he called the coast guard to make a report. As he waited for the duty officer to come on the line, he watched Ruth talking to Dwayne, her voice low and soothing, the talk punctuated regularly with quick smiles; and when finally he was able to report what he'd seen, carefully replaying it, describing the two separate explosions, he suddenly wondered how much emptier Dwayne's eyes would be when he eventually learned that the boat had been deliberately sunk.

When he got back into the truck, Ruth looked at him questioningly.

"I told them that we're cold and wet," he explained, "and that we wanted something to eat." Using one outstretched finger, he tapped Dwayne on the knee, then when he had his attention, he tapped himself on the chest. "Skinny can make a pizza, partner." He shifted his glance to Ruth. "They said to go on home, and they'd send a man by. I gave them your address—it's closer."

Ruth nodded slightly, accepting that, and as soon as Skinny put the truck in gear, she began her soothing talk again, somehow knowing instinctively just what to say—somehow making Skinny feel awkward and a little excluded as she showed him a part of her he had never before seen.

4

When Skinny had been in the fifth grade, before the spurt of growth that had left him skinny rather than just thin, he had lived with his parents in Gentilly, a working-class residential area located between New Orleans's downtown and the Industrial Canal. It was at about that age that Skinny had discovered baseball—and the advantages a baseball bat gave to many of his social relations—and it had been, overall, a very pleasant time in his life. In the mornings, his mother had given him breakfast before he had ridden his bike off to school, where he had tolerated classes while awaiting recess and gym; and after school, he had gone either to the ball field to play baseball or to the canal to explore the highly industrialized ship-building area with its dry docks and cranes, huge tools and mountainous piles of metal scrap. Most Saturdays, his father had taken him fishing. And as Skinny unloaded his truck in front of Ruth's apartment, taking out the few pieces of driftwood Ruth had found, getting ready to hose them off, he tried to recapture his frame of mind as a ten-year-old, remembering his bicycle, his aquarium, his room in his parents' small house, trying

21

to understand how Dwayne must feel but knowing that he never would, not really.

"He's exhausted," Ruth said, coming outside as Skinny put down the last piece of driftwood. "He fell asleep as soon as he lay down."

"The boat was sunk on purpose," Skinny replied, jumping right to what was bothering him most. He went past Ruth to the side of the house, turned on the spigot, came back trailing the hose.

"Are you sure of that?" Ruth asked calmly, knowing Skinny well enough to know that he sometimes jumped to conclusions he amended a short while later, after he had thought things out.

Skinny adjusted the nozzle on the hose, momentarily spraying himself before he was able to focus the water into a stream. He glanced at Ruth uncertainly, then he shrugged, raising and dropping both his shoulders at once.

"Pretty sure," he admitted. He moved the stream of water back and forth over the nearest piece of driftwood. "A few years ago, the captain sent me to school rather than put me on suspension—he said he thought I should be in charge of bomb disposal."

Ruth grinned at that because Skinny was the least likely person she could imagine to *choose* to handle explosives; but as soon as she thought it, she saw the captain's reasoning: if there *was* a way to calm Skinny down, maybe it was with a stick of dynamite.

"The captain thought that, too," Skinny said sourly, reading Ruth exactly. "It didn't work."

Ruth smiled warmly, then pursed her lips.

"So, anyway," Skinny continued, "Skinny took a week-long course in bombs." He moved the hose to another piece of driftwood. "And from what I saw, the boat was deliberately sunk. The explosion was just made to *look* like an accident to anyone watching from shore."

"What's the point of that?" Ruth asked, sitting down on the front steps, folding her arms on her knees. "When the boat is found—"

"The boat *won't* be found," Skinny interrupted her. With the toe of his boot, he rolled over the first piece of driftwood so he could rinse the underside, too. "Where we were, the river is over two hundred feet deep. There's too much silt in the water for sonar to work. The current is fast—no telling how far down it drifted . . ."

Skinny allowed his words to trail off as he recalled the way the boat had slipped beneath the surface, with hardly a ripple. He was taken by an eerie image of it underwater, stern-down but still moving forward, a ghost ship.

"I nearly drowned my ass in that river," he went on. "Not today. When I was about his age." He jerked his chin toward the house. "I got caught in a whirlpool, a big one. It was like riding a merry-go-round, except that it kept going down. I still don't know how I got out of it."

Ruth ran her hand through her hair and held it pulled straight back from her forehead.

"That's terrifying," she said.

"It scared the shit out of Skinny," Skinny agreed. He started to say something else, to explain why he knew the boat had been purposely sunk, but he saw a car turn at the corner, coming their way.

It's not Skinny's problem anyway, he said to himself, moving the hose to the third, and last, piece of driftwood. *This lucky bastard can handle it.*

The unmarked government car that came down the block was dark blue, American-made, and very square, with dull, faded paint and oversized tires that identified it as plainly as a shield-shaped decal on the door. It came forward slowly, then stopped in front of the driveway. The man who got out had a large nose, small eyes, and a very high forehead that led up to curly, reddish brown hair. He wore a short-sleeved white wash-and-wear shirt with a thin tie, loose at the collar. He was a large man, solidly built but gone a bit soft. He smiled over the car, tentatively, the skin crinkling around the corners of his eyes.

"You made the call?" he asked.

Skinny nodded, and the man reached back into the car, turned off the ignition, and came out with an aluminum clipboard.

Skinny turned off the hose by twisting the nozzle.

"My name is Gatzke," the man said, coming around the front of the car. "If you made the report, I know who you are." He smiled again, a thin, friendly smile.

"This is Skinny," Skinny said anyway. "That's Ruth."

Gatzke nodded to them both, then looked at his clipboard.

"You reported that you saw a boat explode and sink in mile sixteen from the Carrollton gauge—"

"In Catfish Bend," Skinny interjected.

"Same place," Gatzke explained. "Mile sixteen is the coast guard designation for Catfish Bend." He looked from Skinny to Ruth, feeling her questioning gaze on him.

"You don't look like you're from the coast guard," Ruth said apologetically. "I guess I expected someone wearing a uniform."

"Oh," Gatzke replied right away. "Sorry." He reached into his shirt pocket, behind the pens that were clipped there, and took out a small wallet. He tucked the clipboard under one arm, removed two business cards from the wallet, stepped forward, and handed one card to Ruth and one to Skinny. Then he stepped back almost shyly.

"Alcohol, Tobacco, and Firearms?" Ruth read aloud from the card, making it a question with her tone.

"All the good stuff," Gatzke replied with earnest good humor. After a moment, he went on. "About a mile upriver from Catfish Bend, there's something called an 'explosive anchorage.' It's where ships are parked if they're carrying hazardous or unstable cargo, anything that might explode. Parking them there keeps them at a safe distance from other ships in the area—there's a navy ship at the anchorage now that's carrying munitions. You reported a boat exploding nearby, you made the coast guard nervous. Weapons and explosives are our jurisdiction, so they passed the buck to us." He took the clipboard from under his arm. "It's Sunday," he added with a genial shrug. "I had the beeper." He brought the clipboard up and glanced at the form clipped to the top of it. "You were out collecting driftwood, and you saw a boat explode. Is that right?"

"Yes," Ruth replied.

"What happened then?"

"We were looking right at it," Ruth began, and while she recounted what had happened, Skinny went over and idly looked in the passenger-side window of Gatzke's car, cupping his hands against the glass; then he examined the car's body, curiously inspecting the paint. Brushing his hands, he turned back as Ruth finished her account, explaining that the boy was inside the house.

"It wasn't an accident," Skinny stated flatly. "The boat was deliberately sunk." He leaned back against the car and crossed his arms on his chest. "The damage to the deck was directional. The explosion on the stern blew down, down and out, somewhere below the waterline; the pilot house blew *up*. It wasn't a secondary explosion. I'm positive about that. There were two separate charges."

Gatzke stopped writing and looked up, squinting in a way that showed his surprise.

"I took the FBI short course in bombs," Skinny explained.

"He's a policeman," Ruth added.

"Jesus Christ," Skinny said.

"Jesus Christ," Gatzke repeated, under his breath.

But Skinny heard him. So did Ruth.

"You might have mentioned that before," Gatzke said. He opened the back of the clipboard and took out another form, which he stepped forward and handed to Skinny. "You would've saved me a lot of writing."

"Skinny's not too big on writing himself," Skinny said, reviewing the elaborate form for a "supplemental officer's report."

"You can type it," Gatzke offered.

"Terrific," Skinny remarked.

"Ruth will type it," Ruth volunteered.

Skinny folded the form then folded it again and slid it into his still-damp hip pocket.

Although he kept his thin smile in place, Gatzke's face took on a pained look as he watched how his report form was treated.

"There's something else, too," Skinny went on, realizing an ATF agent would be interested in the gun he had seen. "Something else I saw on the boat. I found a pistol—I've never seen one like it before."

Gatzke suddenly found something to write on his clipboard, a response that Skinny found curious.

"Yeah?" he said.

"Yeah. It was a little bigger than a Colt automatic, and it had a select firing capability. The receiver housing was glass reinforced, some kind of plastic. Gas-operated, locked-breech, small caliber but high velocity, probably a centerfire."

"What did you do with it?" Gatzke asked, still writing, checking over his form.

"I left it on the boat," Skinny replied. "I sure wasn't going for a swim with it."

Gatzke looked up with a helpless, almost irritated, what-do-you-want-me-to-do-about-it expression, an expression that made Skinny even more curious.

"Have you ever seen a pistol like it?"

"No," Gatzke replied, smiling his tentative smile again, like the one he had used when he had first pulled up. But he had. He had seen one. Skinny was sure of it. He saw it in the sudden, veiled hardness in Gatzke's eyes and in the way his widely spaced eyebrows went up a fraction too high.

"I just thought I'd mention it," Skinny said, not pressing it, knowing there could be any number of reasons why Gatzke would not want to acknowledge the gun.

It's not my problem, Skinny repeated to himself, though he decided right then that he didn't like Gatzke a bit.

"Everything helps," Gatzke said. "Be sure to put it in your report."

"I'll put it in my report, all right," Skinny said, his tone hard enough to make Gatzke look up from his clipboard. His glance was speculative, speculative and not very friendly.

"Where do you suppose they were going?" Ruth asked. "Down somewhere people didn't speak English?"

When Gatzke looked at Ruth, his eyes changed in a blink.

"That's the sixty-four-dollar question," he replied easily. "My guess is, they were headed to somewhere around

Lafayette. Acadiana is only a couple of hundred miles from here, and there are places around there where people speak French." He shrugged, smiling reassuringly as he did so. "We'll find out when we find out who blew up the boat." He put both his hands on his hips, holding the clipboard in one thick fist, allowing it to lean against the inside of his forearm; then he scratched his upper arm, using his knuckles. "You want to keep the boy?" he asked Ruth.

"Keep him?" Ruth replied, taken aback.

Gatzke adjusted his shirt sleeve.

"Not keep him, exactly. Get him home, to his aunt."

Gatzke's face showed a solicitous, squinting concern Skinny found vaguely disgusting. He knew what Gatzke was up to, trying to save himself a lot of paperwork by not taking the boy into custody, but he didn't know what to do about it, not now that he was playing to Ruth.

"If I take him," he went on, "I have to put him in a youth home until someone comes to get him." When Ruth did not seem to understand, he explained, "I have to take him to a detention center. I can't just hold him—he'll be locked up with juvenile offenders."

"My God," Ruth began heatedly. "What kind of—?"

"We'll get him home," Skinny said.

Gatzke grinned at Skinny, then gave Ruth an unconvincing I-don't-make-the-rules shrug. He made a final notation on his clipboard.

"As soon as you have the boy home, call me at the number on my card." He looked up, smiling again. "And don't forget the report."

Skinny refused to acknowledge that in any way at all.

Gatzke glanced first at Skinny, then at Ruth; then he went to his car and got in, stopping only long enough to examine the smudges Skinny had left on the windows.

He made a face he made sure Skinny saw, then he drove off, his lips pursed as if he were whistling.

"I don't like that man," Ruth said. She put her hands in her hip pockets, palms flat against her hips in a tense stance that conveyed her barely restrained anger. "I don't like his attitude."

"That's one way to put it," Skinny remarked, and began to coil up the hose. "Skinny'd get a little more personal."

"He reminds me of the basketball coach we had in high school." Ruth was still looking off, down the block, her eyes on the corner where Gatzke had turned. "He kicked things when we were losing."

Skinny stopped in midcoil.

"*You* played basketball?"

Ruth shot him a warning glance.

"Don't start, Skinny," she said, just aggravated enough to mean it.

"Jesus Christ," Skinny said, and without another word he finished coiling the hose.

5

As soon as she had warned Skinny not to start, Ruth felt bad that she had been short with him; but she was at that moment too preoccupied to apologize right away. She was angry about a policy that did not differentiate between a juvenile offender and a juvenile victim, and she was concerned about the boy, about Dwayne. She went inside to check on him, allowing the screen door to slam shut behind her.

Dwayne was asleep on her bed, just where she had left him, the light quilt she had put over him now thrown off to one side. She replaced the quilt, carefully tucking it up under his chin, then sat down in the chair beside the bed, alternately looking at Dwayne and looking out the window, trying to sort out her thoughts. She heard Skinny come inside, use the phone in the kitchen, then go into the living room and turn on the last few minutes of the game.

Ruth was, overall, reasonably pleased with her life. She had a new job as the head of a typing pool that seemed to be working out well. She and Skinny, it seemed, were growing together, now more than just casual lovers—and thanks to Skinny, for the first time in her life she had a little money invested. Ruth liked her apartment. She liked the small routines in her day. She liked the freedom her own self-sufficiency brought her. In a way, she supposed, she was selfish because she was concerned primarily about herself, about getting by; but she forgave herself pretty readily because the getting by so often took so much of her energy.

Dwayne moaned in his sleep and twisted around, kicking the quilt off his feet.

Ruth saw that he still had on his sneakers.

Almost all the women with whom Ruth had gone to high school were married. Most had been married a long time—some, the early starters, had children in high school themselves. And as her mother often reminded her, if she ever wanted children herself, she had better get started.

"If I feel the urge to have children," Ruth invariably replied, "I'll go out and get myself a cocker spaniel puppy."

But it wasn't that she didn't want children, not ever, it was that she didn't see how she could have children and maintain her self-sufficiency, too—in her mind, one necessarily preceded the other.

Dwayne moved again, rolling onto his back.

When Ruth was thirteen years old, when she had reached her most gangly and had been most painfully aware of herself, of her gawky height, her clumsiness, the cat's-eye glasses that she was sure made her look like a bean pole wearing reflectors, her father had left. She remembered his leaving very clearly. She remembered how, when he had come into her room to say good-bye, he had put his suitcase down by the door; she remembered the seeming finality of the clicks the suitcase's metal feet had made on the floor. And she remembered how, thinking that she was asleep, he had bent down and kissed her on the cheek. She remembered his touch and the way he had smelled; but what she remembered even more clearly were the months that had followed before he had come back, the paralyzing panic her mother had felt, the clammy fear.

Ruth crossed her long legs, took a cigarette from her pocket and lit it, squinting her eyes at the smoke.

Her mother had had no skills, really—she had never held a real job. She had gotten married right out of high school, and she had for so long been so totally dependent that, left to herself, she had had no notion at all of what to do to get on with her life. Ruth remembered how her mother had clutched her later that same morning, holding to her for way too long, and she remembered her mother's long, vacant stares, the hours she had just sat, overwhelmed. She remembered the meals forgotten, the phones left endlessly ringing, the bills left unpaid— though even at the time she had known that it wasn't just money that was causing her mother's despair. And right then, at her gawkiest and least confident, Ruth had promised herself never to let the same thing happen to her, never to become too dependent on anyone else, a promise she had kept, as she viewed it now, with perhaps too much enthusiasm.

Ruth picked up the ashtray she kept beside the bed and held it in one hand, tapping the ash on her cigarette over it. She looked at Dwayne, feeling a warmth and an uncertainty—and a peculiar, clear strength.

There was a distinction to be made between commitment and dependence, a lesson she realized she was only beginning to learn. There was a balance to be struck, a middle ground.

In the mirror over her dresser, Ruth caught a glimpse

of herself, the corners of her mouth turned down, her brow furrowed, looking so serious. She made a quick, humorous face in the mirror, then put out her cigarette and stood up to go into the next room.

Before she left, she pulled the quilt back over Dwayne.

Skinny was standing up, bent at the waist, his arms straight out behind him, poised as if to dive, heavily involved in the game. Something happened that obviously stunned him, and he let out a soundless yowl. He jerked up straight as if he had been stuck with a pin.

Ruth noticed that he had taken off his boots and had the volume turned low.

A commercial came on, and he picked up his soda from the top of the TV and took a long swallow, noticing in mid-drink that Ruth was behind him. He froze, his eyes cut back at her, and the syrupy liquid sloshed down his chin. He wiped at his mouth with the back of his hand.

"I like football," he explained.

"I would never have guessed," Ruth replied, smiling.

Skinny glanced at the TV, then back at Ruth.

"I called the Silver Lily, the club where Dwayne's aunt works." He shrugged. "Nobody's home."

"How about if Ruth makes the pizza?" Ruth asked.

"How about," Skinny replied, sensing that something was up with Ruth but distracted by the game. He snuck a look at the television, just for a moment, but when he looked back, Ruth was already gone.

6

After Dwayne had awakened and Ruth had finished cooking the pizza, while they were eating Skinny had again called the Silver Lily Club, and this time someone had been there: he had been given the message that Dwayne's aunt was at home. Skinny had said to tell her that they would meet her at the club. So after they had eaten, Skinny drove Dwayne and Ruth back across the Mississippi River Bridge, taking the same route Ruth and he had taken that morning when they had set out for driftwood; but once on the west bank he turned upriver rather than downriver and got on the elevated expressway. They went through, practically over, Gretna and Harvey and got off the expressway where it ended in Marrero. And although they were only seven miles from New Orleans's downtown, the dilapidated, mostly vacant houses in the area seemed to bear no relation at all to the bright lights in the distance. The one streetlight in that part of Marrero cast a pocket of harsh orange light against the graffiti-covered wall of a desolate playground. All around there were cars up on blocks. A dead tree lay where it had fallen along the curb. Skinny and Ruth stayed near Skinny's truck. Dwayne was not far away, in the pool of bright light that illuminated the Silver Lily Club's entrance.

"Have you thought about whether or not you ever want children?" Ruth asked.

Skinny swiveled his head around and looked right at her.

"Where did *that* come from?" he replied, taken aback.

"It's not totally out of the blue," Ruth observed, looking around, both amazed and saddened at how much farther they had come than the distance alone would indicate. "It's something to think about," she added.

"I'm thinking," Skinny said, again looking around himself, concerned about their safety in that neighborhood.

Dwayne idly kicked the faded wood building, watching as pieces of rotted wood fell onto the ground.

Skinny took out the piece of gum he had been chewing, rolled it into a ball, threw it away. He glanced at Ruth.

"I'm still thinking," he said.

Ruth smiled at that.

"It's not like you have to decide in the next two minutes," she noted.

"That's a relief," Skinny remarked, crossing his arms on his chest.

Suddenly, Dwayne looked up and bolted, running out of the light.

Alarmed, Skinny moved after him, but right after he started, he stopped abruptly, seeing a lone figure coming down the levee and Dwayne running toward it.

Ruth bumped into his back.

"Sorry," she said. "Be careful," she added, and together they set out to meet Dwayne's aunt.

The woman who came down the levee was older than Skinny had expected, in her midfifties at least. She was a large woman with big hips, big breasts, and large fleshy arms. She wore a faded dress with broad, vertical stripes, and although it was hard to see in the dim light, still Skinny could discern the family resemblance to Dwayne in her small ears set close to her head.

"This is Skinny," Skinny said. "This is Ruth."

"I'm Agnes Charles," the woman replied. "Dwayne's aunt." She had one hand on Dwayne's shoulder, holding him close to her side.

"There was an accident," Ruth began. "The boat—"

"I know," Agnes Charles interrupted her with a kind smile. "A policeman called when I passed by the club." There was sadness in her voice, but there was a solid strength, too, a strength that suggested other losses suffered, and survived. "The boy will be fine with me—I take care of him mostly anyway. Isn't that right, Dwayne?" She gave Dwayne's shoulder a squeeze.

Dwayne did not reply but held to her leg.

"The policeman said you pulled Dwayne out the water."

"Skinny's a good swimmer," Skinny replied, shrugging offhandedly.

"Lucky you are, too. Lucky you were there. This boy ain't no kind of swimmer at all." Agnes gave Dwayne another squeeze, looking at him, and when she looked up, she looked right at Skinny. "Thank you. I know you did all you could."

Skinny did not know how to reply to that, so he did not reply at all. An awkward silence followed in which it became apparent that there was nothing more to say.

"I'll take the boy home now," Agnes Charles said finally. "Put him to bed."

Ruth bent down and rubbed Dwayne's arm, shoulder to elbow, then she stood back up and put her hands in her pockets.

Skinny waved.

Agnes smiled, then she and Dwayne turned away and started up the levee.

Ruth and Skinny both watched them a moment before they turned, too, and went the opposite direction. Ruth brought out a tissue and dabbed at her eyes.

Skinny said, "For Christ's sake," in a way that made Ruth smile. She took Skinny's hand as they walked back to the truck. Before they were there, they heard a gas-powered generator start up and begin to hammer.

"Is that how they get electricity?" Ruth asked. "From a generator?"

Skinny nodded as he opened the door to his truck.

"They'd have to. It's illegal to live on the batture—the power company wouldn't hook them up."

On the other side of the levee, the generator seemed to lose its rhythm and popped loudly.

Ruth cocked an ear at the sound. So did Skinny.

"It sounds like it's running out of gas," Ruth observed.

Skinny shut the door to the truck.

"I have gas. There's a can in back—I just filled it."

The gas can was secured to the bed of the truck by a chain through its handle. Skinny dug in his pocket for the key, but he stopped, his hand still in his pocket, when the popping sounds came again. He brought out the key, unlocked the chain, pulled out the gas can.

Ruth was five steps ahead, waiting impatiently.

Carrying the three-gallon can of gas, Skinny walked more slowly than he usually did, leaning into the effort, and by the time he reached the foot of the levee, the generator had settled down to a reassuringly steady, hammering drone that made him wonder whether or not they should cross the levee at all.

"This may not be such a good idea," he began. "It—"

"It'll just take a minute," Ruth cut him off, and from the way that she said it, Skinny knew she was determined to go.

"You want to see the house, right?"

"Right," Ruth affirmed readily.

"Come back tomorrow," he said, but Ruth was already moving away, up the levee and over the top.

"Damn," Skinny said, and switched the gas can to his other hand. "Shit," he said, when gas sloshed onto his jeans.

From the top of the levee, a path lead across the batture, through the trees, to a rickety wooden walkway where Ruth stopped.

"My God," she said softly as Skinny came up beside her, her eyes fixed on the house. "My God."

Although it was lit only by dim yellow bulbs that glowed feebly, still it was obvious that the house was nothing more than a shack, a crude structure that had been patched together on the remnants of an abandoned pier. The walls were made from irregularly cut plywood, old cypress planks, boards of various widths—whatever materials, it was obvious, that had been readily available or had washed up on shore. The roof was old sheets of tin. The generator sat to one side of the house, in front, near where the walkway intersected the pier.

"Hello," Skinny shouted, and put down the gas can. "Hello."

Inside the shack, behind the white sheet that served as a curtain, a shadow flicked past, a quick movement.

A screen door screeched open and slammed shut.

Outside, there was another furtive movement.

"Hello," Skinny shouted again.

An outboard motor cranked and coughed but failed to fire.

Skinny started up the walkway to the pier. Before he had gone three steps, he heard the same sharp pops Ruth and he had heard a few minutes before, but with them now there were splotches of bright yellow flame, gunshots, not sputters, sharp, fast reports. Behind him, bullets smacked into wet earth.

"Holy shit," he said, and dove off the walkway, banging his shin on the gas can, grabbing Ruth as he went past her, pulling her down into the weeds. He let go of Ruth, clutched his shin, and at the same time unzipped his jacket, taking out his silver gun, a complicated combination of movements that worked his shoulder down into the mud.

The outboard motor caught and revved high, a frantic, gurgling whine.

"You stay here," Skinny whispered to Ruth, his tone insistent.

Ruth nodded slightly.

"I mean it."

The outboard's gears gnashed, and it was apparent the operator was fumbling, trying to get the motor in gear.

Crouched low, favoring his sore leg, Skinny made his way back to the walkway and went up it, moving in spurts, taking a few steps, stopping, moving again. At the top of the walkway he stretched out, chest and thighs against the rough boards. He low-crawled toward the still-hammering generator and got behind it; and just then he heard the outboard motor rev high again, droning, in gear now, pulling away.

"Shit," he said, and rolled out from behind the generator, silver gun cocked and extended, too late to do more than watch the small boat disappear on the river.

He stood up quickly and went to the front of the house, quietly edging his way to the door. He glanced in once before he threw open the screen door and slipped through it.

The room was still and empty, modestly furnished but neat, neat and clean. The chair behind which he crouched faced a sofa; to the left of the sofa was the door to another room.

"Hello," he called out. "Hello. This is Skinny," and he swung around the chair, silver gun clutched in both hands.

In the next room, there was a large bed on the right and a folding army-style cot on the left, both neatly made up; between the bed and the cot was a small chest of drawers and a large, overstuffed chair. Agnes Charles was slumped down in the chair, her head resting in the corner formed by the wing and the back, a large, dark stain slowly spreading across the front of her dress. Skinny moved past her to the back door, quickly opened it and looked out, returned to kneel down beside her.

Agnes Charles felt Skinny lift her wrist, searching for a pulse, and she moved slightly, shaking her head when he put one arm behind her knees, getting ready to lift her, to lay her out on the floor. Her eyes opened slightly, her lids heavy, and Skinny saw in her face great dignity, dignity and, even then, calm strength; then very slowly the light dimmed and went out in her eyes.

Skinny gently removed his arm and rocked back, sitting down on his heels, not yet able to think, not able to sort out what had happened. After a few moments, he picked up his silver gun where he had put it on the floor. He started to stand up, but a cold feeling stopped him; he glanced up and saw Ruth standing in the doorway, frozen, her eyes too wide open, her face colorless and drawn, a stunned, brittle mask.

"Jesus Christ," he said very softly, and quickly moved to her, purposely blocking her view of Agnes Charles's body.

Ruth looked at him, seemingly without recognition, her eyes overloaded. When Skinny put his hands on her shoulders, she allowed him to turn her and to lead her outside.

The broad expanse of the Mississippi River was inky blackness. Single lights' reflections and, farther down-river, a whole galaxy of lights and colors from downtown smeared across the water's rough surface. The generator droned steadily; soothing lapping sounds came up from beneath the pier. The air was cool and smelled of the river.

Ruth was leaning back against the cluster of pilings at the very end of the pier. Skinny was standing next to her.

"We have to go call the police," he said. "We have to make a report."

Ruth did not look away from the river.

"You go," she said. "I'll wait here."

Skinny started to argue with her, but when he saw the faraway look in her eyes, he decided to give her the time to herself—it seemed extremely unlikely to him that the killer would return.

"I'll be as quick as I can," he said, but he was still reluctant to leave her. "Are you okay?"

Ruth nodded, then looked back at him, away from the

shiny, black river. Her eyes were no longer faraway but right there, right there and extremely hard.

"You find that little boy," she said, a chilling edge on her words. "You find that little boy, and you find the man who killed that poor woman."

7

Skinny hurried back across the levee and, because he wasn't familiar with the area, to the Silver Lily Club, which was the only place nearby where he knew for certain that there was a phone. Since he was preoccupied with what had happened, still hearing the edge on Ruth's words, not really noticing what otherwise he might have, it was only after he had rushed inside the club, flinging the door open wide, that he realized what he had stepped into.

Oh, boy, he said to himself, quickly looking around, hoping the phone was readily at hand. "Sorry," he said as he squeezed past the man at the door.

Even though it was Sunday evening, the Silver Lily Club was crowded, crowded and bustling. Cigar and cigarette smoke made a haze in the air. On the left, a long bar ran the length of the room, and at it the predominantly male crowd was gathered in loose groups, each group with a woman or two at its center. On the right, there were red vinyl booths. The floor was covered with linoleum. Behind the bar, behind the rows of liquor bottles in tiers, the wall was covered with gold-veined mirrored squares. Small lamps with pink, rosy bulbs were affixed to the same wall, and in the mirrors Skinny saw that the light seemed to make him pink, too, in disconcertingly high contrast to the black men and women around him: he was the only white person in the place, and it was readily obvious he was not welcome. As his rosy pink presence was noticed, conversation dwindled and became ominously forced. The noise level dropped appreciably.

Skinny shrugged and smiled brightly, and made his way to the bar.

The bartender eyed Skinny coldly, then studiously ignored him as he continued to mix drinks. When he put two drinks up on the bar nearby, Skinny said, "I need to use the phone," rather genially for Skinny.

The bartender went on as he had before, simply pretending that he hadn't heard him, mixing more drinks; but Skinny saw his eyes, hidden in the folds of his dark, fleshy face, glance to the left, to the back of the room. In the end booth, a man nodded slightly, barely perceptibly, and after a moment the bartender brought a phone, which he gruffly sat on the bar.

Immediately, conversation began to pick up again.

"Thanks," Skinny said, wondering whether or not he could ask for a soda, but the bartender moved away before he had his thirst relative to his situation fully considered.

Skinny called the police, and because he was in a neighboring parish, he explained who he was before he explained what had happened; and he tried to call Agent Gatzke, but a recording informed him that the ATF office was closed. Just to cover himself, he called his own office, too, and as he made all the calls, whenever he could without being too obvious, he glanced back at the man in the end booth.

The man was very dark-skinned, and in the dim light his features were hard to discern. He was big, though, there was no doubt about that, big and powerful, at least twice as wide as the woman beside him. Wrapped around a tall can of beer, his hands looked big enough to drive fence posts. His eyes were black and full of energy, often in motion, glancing around. He wore a rust-red suit and white shirt. Behind and above him, on top of the booth-bench, a large, brightly colored bird paced back and forth, stopping only when the man casually reached up and handed him a treat, a piece of pretzel or chip. Once or twice the bird squawked for more.

Skinny finished making his calls and left the Silver Lily, grateful to the man but knowing better than to thank him, briefly entertaining the notion of getting a big bird for himself.

The police arrived and established a crime scene that included the whole pier and a broad section of levee. Skinny watched critically, making more than a few suggestions, as high-intensity lights were brought in and Agnes Charles's shack was lit up as brightly as if they were making a movie.

Ruth stayed down on the end of the pier.

Before the coroner arrived, one technician videotaped the whole scene, and another took color pictures. A detective sketched a floor plan that showed the angles from which the pictures were taken. Officers in uniform held back the onlookers who had formed a crowd at the base of the levee. With all the activity, Skinny didn't notice when his partner, Mike Theriot, arrived and went up to Ruth.

Mike Theriot had been in the detective bureau just over a year, long enough to feel confident of his job, though Skinny still thought he was nervous. He was dark-complexioned, not very tall, and parted his black hair on the side, allowing it to fall across one side of his forehead at an angle. He wore an army-blanket green suit and wide, one-color tie that matched the suit exactly. He carried a cheap chrome flashlight that was over two feet long. When working, by an order from the chief of detectives issued in an effort both to protect police cars and to save Skinny his job, Mike Theriot and Skinny shared a car, even when they were working different cases. Mike Theriot drove. Skinny gave directions.

Ruth was very pleased to see him.

"So this is how you two make a living," she said when he came up, nodding toward the shack and all the activity, naturally including Skinny.

Mike Theriot saw the strain in Ruth in her tense expression.

"Skinny called the office and ran it down to me," he replied somberly. He and Skinny had met Ruth at the same time, and although he normally felt very comfortable with her, just then he did not know quite what to say. "I'm sorry, Ruth," he added.

Ruth started to say, "It's not your fault," but before she had the words out, her thoughts skipped ahead. "I don't know how you do it." She nodded again, toward the shack. "How do you go to work knowing . . . ?" She ran her hand through her hair and glanced out at the river. "My God, we'd just met that poor woman." Her thoughts were full of feeling but fragmented, coming too quickly. "Who would want to kill her? What could she possibly have that they'd want that badly?" After a while, she glanced back. "The boy has disappeared."

Mike Theriot thought about what Ruth had just said, his brow furrowed earnestly, and decided to answer the question she had left unfinished.

"You know what I do?" he said. "When it gets really

rough?" He waited until his eyes caught Ruth's. "I think about something else." He tapped his flashlight against the side of his leg. "It drives Skinny nuts. There we'll be, in the middle of a crime scene, and when I want to I just daydream my way out of there."

Ruth smiled because she knew that that was, without doubt, exactly the sort of thing that would drive Skinny right up a wall.

"You remember the day we got the reward?" Mike Theriot went on, referring to the reward the three of them had split for finding out who had burned down a warehouse. "Skinny took us fishing." He shook his head side to side slowly. "I still can't get over it. To celebrate, he took us *fishing*." He held his flashlight in both hands and flexed his wrists against it, as if trying to bend it. "Anyway, I think about something like that."

"And *we* went," Ruth reminded him, for a moment recalling that day herself. She remembered the bright sun and the heat, and the way the spray from the bayou had felt on her face. She remembered the pelican they had seen and the alligator that had almost caught it.

"It nearly killed Skinny that you got the only fish."

"The only one we could *keep*," Ruth corrected him.

"I'm not counting that little minnow he pulled in and said was a redfish."

Ruth's smile broadened when she recalled Skinny's triumphant expression when the fish had taken his line and his pouting look of disappointment when he had pulled the fish out of the water.

"Too bad it's a redfish," he had said, holding up his small trophy. "We have to throw it back."

"You can keep it if you want," Mike Theriot had retorted. "You put it in with a can of sardines, and nobody'll notice the difference."

"I thought he was going to throw you overboard," Ruth observed.

"I thought he was going to *shoot* me," Mike Theriot said. "I think I took my life in my hands."

Ruth was about to laugh at that, but just then the door to the shack opened and the coroner's assistants came out with Agnes Charles's body. Unable to use a gurney on the irregular boards that made up the pier, they were having to carry her. Four of them were struggling with the weight in the black plastic bag.

Mike Theriot grimaced, sorry about the timing, sorry that Ruth would not get even a momentary relief from the strain she was obviously feeling.

Ruth crossed her arms and again turned to the river. Out on the water, a huge freighter was gliding past soundlessly, going downriver, a looming black shape on the black water. She watched it until only its red and green running lights were visible, and then the lights, too, faded away. Behind her, she heard Skinny say to Mike Theriot, "The lab vacuumed the place until the floor nails were coming up. Trace evidence is already on its way in."

Mike Theriot asked, his voice low, "What about the boy?"

Ruth could almost hear Skinny shrug.

"The only thing Skinny knows for sure is that he wasn't in the boat. He saw that much. One man."

Mike Theriot suppressed the obvious question. His flashlight rattled as he tapped it against the side of his leg.

"I'm going home," he said. "It's been a long day."

"Us, too," Skinny replied. "A real long day," he agreed, glancing at Ruth. "You ready to go?"

Ruth nodded silently.

The three of them went down the walkway and up over the levee, past the crowd of onlookers, which had thinned out considerably once the body had been removed.

8

The rule taught in countersurveillance class was, make three right turns if you think you are being followed.

So after he spotted the dark blue Chevrolet, Skinny made the suggested three turns, driving no more erratically than he normally did, trying to determine whether or not they were, indeed, being followed.

Ruth did not seem to notice the impromptu tour of the Westwego neighborhood but sat quietly, just looking out.

Skinny had first noticed the car when they had left the parking lot near the Silver Lily Club, and now, the third turn completed, satisfied that the car was, in fact, behind him, he drove straight to the expressway and headed for New Orleans.

"What was that for?" Ruth asked, mildly curious, belatedly remarking on Skinny's slight detour.

"I wanted to see if we were being followed," Skinny replied. He glanced in the rearview mirror, putting his face right in front of it, then ran both his hands through his hair, as if he had used the mirror only to check his appearance. "We are," he added happily.

Ruth started to glance behind them, but when Skinny let go of the wheel, the truck veered to the right, onto the shoulder, and instead she grabbed the wheel.

"Thanks," Skinny said, taking it back.

"Who is following us?" Ruth asked.

"Skinny's thought about this one," Skinny remarked, not answering the question. He smiled smugly, a devious gleam in his eyes. "He knows right where to take 'em."

"But who are they, Skinny?"

Skinny shrugged.

"We'll find out soon enough, that's for sure."

Ruth put her arm along the top of the seat and surreptitiously glanced back just as Skinny changed lanes and sped up, beginning to cut in and out of traffic, picking up the pace.

Ruth jerked to one side, then the other.

The Chevrolet stayed right behind them.

Skinny said, "Did you know that those big parrots you see sometimes live to be over a hundred years old? They can learn about seventy-five words, sometimes more— more than a German shepherd." He paused, then added, "More than Theriot."

Ruth did not say anything but waited, knowing Skinny well enough to know that he would soon make a connection.

"I saw a parrot in the Silver Lily when I went in to use the phone," Skinny explained a few moments later. "I'm thinking about getting one for myself."

Ruth immediately pictured Skinny with a parrot on his shoulder, one strange, gawky bird on another, and looked to the front, hoping Skinny would not see her smile.

"What's so funny about that?" Skinny wanted to know.

"I've heard that they're very expensive," Ruth replied, hoping that that would throw him off.

"Yeah?" Skinny said guardedly, looking over skeptically though obviously concerned, curious enough not to notice the car right in front of them. "How much do they cost?"

Before Ruth could reply, Skinny saw the car and swerved, cutting neatly around it. He smiled, pleased with himself.

"Anyway, I'll price 'em."

"You watch your driving," Ruth warned. When Skinny held steady on an open stretch of expressway, she glanced back at the car following, seeing it very clearly in the orange light from the light standards, seeing, behind its headlights, the two black men inside it.

"They still with us?" Skinny said.

"Yes. What do you think they want, Skinny? Who are they?"

There was concern in Ruth's tone, but it was a mild concern, tempered by Skinny's apparent nonchalance.

"I don't know who they are," Skinny replied, "but I can make a pretty good guess what they want." He twisted around on the seat so that he was leaning back into the corner formed by the seat and the door. His eyes flicked from the road to the mirror to Ruth. "First, this afternoon we call the Silver Lily and leave messages, then this evening we show up with the boy. We meet with Agnes Charles. A while later, I show up again to use the phone. The police come. Agnes Charles has been shot. From out of nowhere, suddenly we're all over the place. If I were in their shoes, I'd want to know who the shit *we* are."

Ruth's expression became slightly unfocused as she mulled that over, and she did not seem ready to make the leap to the question Skinny thought she should ask next, which was, Who was organized enough to have them followed on short notice? So he went on. Not far ahead, the toll plaza for the Mississippi River Bridge came into view.

"When I was in uniform, for a while I worked in the housing projects—they do that to everybody, rotate them through the projects, so they'll know what they're like." He saw Ruth's questioning gaze, and he added, "They're the pits. Whoever thought of putting low-income people all in one place should be made to live in one." He glanced at the approaching tollbooths, then dug down in his pocket for a dollar. "A lot goes on in the projects— they're like cities but more concentrated." He squirmed around on the seat, continuing to search the pockets of his jeans, but was unable to find any money. He looked at Ruth.

"I didn't bring my wallet," Ruth noted.

"Anyway," Skinny went on, only then thinking to look for his wallet, finally finding it in a jacket pocket and taking out a bill, "what I'm getting at is, in the projects, depending on what it is you want, there's always somebody to see. If you're running for office, you see one person. You want to borrow money, you see another. Same thing for selling drugs or buying car parts or starting up a poker game. Anything you can think of, there's someone in charge, someone who has the franchise."

As Skinny slowed to pay the toll, Ruth looked at the huge housing project near the foot of the bridge, thinking of all the activities that went on, all the orbits and connections, getting a sense of a world she had passed by often enough but had never stopped to consider.

"These people," Skinny continued, jerking his thumb

back over his shoulder, indicating the car behind them, "most probably work for somebody who has a franchise. We find out who they are, we find out who they work for, we have a lead back to Agnes Charles, or the boat, maybe both—you can bet the two are connected."

Without stopping, Skinny held out his dollar and rolled through the tollbooth.

Ruth said, "I wonder why she lived in that shack? Away from everyone else?" When the answer occurred to her, it brought with it renewed sadness.

"Shit," Skinny said suddenly. His head snapped around as he looked out the rear window. "Shit," he said again. "The dumb bastards turned off."

Ruth glanced back, too, and saw that the dark blue Chevrolet was no longer behind them.

"They didn't come through the tollbooth."

Skinny looked back again, the other way, hanging out the window this time, allowing the truck to drift.

A horn blared.

Ruth knew immediately what Skinny was considering, a U-turn across five lanes of traffic, and she braced herself against the dash.

"Skinny—" she began, not that she thought it would do any good. She felt a coldness run up her spine.

But Skinny surprised her. He came back in the window, pulled the truck into a lane, and proceeded ahead almost calmly—though he did slap his palm against the wheel.

"Damn," he said, "We lost 'em."

"*They* lost *us*," Ruth noted, more than a little relieved.

Skinny tucked his lower lip between his teeth and chewed it absently as he tried to figure it out. He had assumed that the men in the car would follow them until they at least saw where they were going; and since they hadn't, he wasn't sure at all what they *had*, in fact, wanted.

"Too bad," he said to Ruth, shrugging to himself then smiling brightly, confident that he would see the car again. "Skinny was taking them to the parking lot of the Sixth District police station."

9

Although Skinny and Ruth had several times discussed the possibility of living together, they had never actually decided what they were going to do, largely because neither one of them wanted to give up their own apartment. Ruth genuinely liked the space she had made for herself and the independence her own place gave her; Skinny did not want to give up his apartment because, as the resident policeman in a large complex, he got to live rent-free, a deal he could not bring himself to forsake. Besides that, there was a pool. So by tacit agreement, since they both had to work the next day, Skinny was simply going to drop Ruth off at her apartment uptown then go on home himself; but when they turned onto Ruth's block, there was Agent Gatzke in front of Ruth's house, leaning back against the side of his square, blue government car.

"I could do without this completely," Skinny said.

"Maybe he's found out something about Dwayne," Ruth replied, though even as she said it she realized she was exhausted, too, worn down by the events that had come one right after another.

Agent Gatzke was looking up, apparently gazing at the few stars overhead. One arm across his middle, his other hand at his throat, thumb and first finger spread wide, absently he was smoothing down the skin, pulling it taut. He looked over but did not push himself away from the car.

Skinny stopped the truck in the middle of the street.

"Do you have my supplemental report written yet?" Gatzke asked as soon as Skinny got out of the truck. His small mouth stretched into a smile, revealing small teeth—and making it clear he was making a joke. "I got your message," he added.

"Why didn't you come to the scene?" Skinny asked irritably, walking near him.

Gatzke made a quarter turn to face Skinny, rolling his hip on the fender, and dropped his hand so that his arms were crossed on his chest.

"Did you find out anything about Dwayne?" Ruth asked.

"He's here to ask us," Skinny remarked, "since we've been out doing his work."

For a long moment, Gatzke's eyes locked on Skinny's eyes. He was as tall as Skinny but at least fifty pounds heavier, a big, beefy man. Skinny remembered what Ruth had said about him, that he reminded her of a man who liked to kick things when he got angry, and he checked out his shoes, scuffed brown wingtips with thick leather soles.

"He's right," Gatzke said to Ruth. "I'm here to ask you." He pushed himself away from the car and put both his hands in his hip pockets. "So, hey," he said to Skinny, grinning tentatively, changing his approach in a blink, "you never got it wrong before? Followed up one thing when you should have been following another?" He paused. "I was in Baton Rouge when you called, out of range of my beeper. I didn't get your message until two hours after you left it. And Baton Rouge is an hour away. I broke off there as soon as I could and came here to see you first." He pushed forward his elbows in a sort of a shrug. "Here I am."

Skinny rubbed the tips of his fingers against his unshaven chin, trying to decide whether it was the man or his story that bothered him most.

"What's in Baton Rouge?" he asked.

"My ex-wife," Gatzke replied with a pained look.

Jesus Christ, Skinny said to himself.

"I got most of the story from the parish detective assigned to the case," Gatzke went on. "I spoke to him on the radio during my drive in." He shifted his little eyes to Ruth, smiling ruefully. "I guess I should have taken the boy into custody." His eyes went back to Skinny. "Were you able to see the person who shot at you? Anything about him at all?"

Although Skinny had been asked that same question several times already, and had asked it of himself several times more, still he thought back to the glimpse he had had of the boat pulling away from Agnes Charles's pier.

"I was down low, ready to duck bullets. All I saw was the boat, and I didn't see that real well—just enough to see that the boy wasn't in it. There was one man. He had his back turned. It was dark." Skinny raised and dropped both his shoulders at once. "I couldn't even tell you whether the guy was black or white."

Gatzke looked at Ruth, and she shook her head, indicating that she had not seen anything either; then he looked down.

"So now the little monkey is on the loose," he said absently, looking up again, smiling slightly, reflexly, when he caught Ruth's hard gaze. "The shooter wasn't after the aunt, that's my guess. He was after the boy."

"That's my guess, too," Skinny agreed, careful not to look at Ruth, a little defensive because he had held back on telling her.

"Why?" Ruth asked, her tone firm and demanding, just this side of sharp. "Why do you think that?"

"Because it's the only way it fits," Skinny said. "The boy knows something or he's seen something, enough to worry the guy. He tagged along with his father sometimes, right? Bad move. He's a witness. That's why the guy blew up the boat: he wanted to get them both. When that didn't work, he went back at him. The aunt just got in the way."

Ruth seemed to get angry at that speculation. She crossed her arms low, at her waist.

"It's not 'the aunt' or 'the boy,' " she said hotly. Her gaze flicked past Skinny and landed on Gatzke. "Or 'the little monkey.' These are people. They have names."

Gatzke looked at Skinny as if he expected him to reply, but Skinny remained silent, his eyes fixed on Ruth.

"Coming back here, we were followed," Ruth went on. "When we left the parking lot near the Silver Lily Club, two black men followed us as far as the bridge."

"You lost them?" Gatzke asked.

"They turned off," Ruth replied.

Gatzke shook his head uncertainly, obviously unable to make that make sense.

"Let's hope the boy—" he began, then he stopped and started again. "Let's hope Dwayne has sense enough to come to us first." He reached into his pocket and took out his keys. "If he gets in touch with you, call me."

"It's your case," Skinny affirmed. *I've got other problems,* Skinny said to himself, glancing at Ruth, though he was sure most of his problems would be solved by a good night's uninterrupted sleep.

Once again, in a very short time it seemed, Skinny and Ruth watched Gatzke drive off, making the turn at the corner.

"At least he admitted it when he knew he was wrong," Skinny observed.

"I still don't like his attitude," Ruth replied coldly. "I don't like his snide remarks."

"You're tired," Skinny said with certainty. "Things'll look better tomorrow. I guarantee it."

"I know," Ruth agreed, moving her hands up to her upper arms, rubbing herself as if she were cold.

"So you want some company?" Skinny offered.

Ruth thought that over for a moment, then took one of Skinny's hands in hers.

"Yes," she said, smiling slightly. "Ruth would like some company. Maybe Skinny should park his truck," she suggested.

"Maybe," Skinny replied absently. He took a half step toward his truck then stopped, apparently thinking of something else. "I was just wondering," he said, pausing long enough to convey some concern. "I can't remember whether or not you have any beer."

10

The next morning, Skinny overslept. He had meant to get up early, with Ruth, so that he could go home and shower before Theriot came to get him for work; but by the time the alarm clock's persistent buzzer had awakened him, Ruth was already gone and he was late.

"Damn," he said, and rolled out of bed to turn off the alarm. "Shit," he said when he tripped over his boots.

He dressed hurriedly and straightened the bed, making it after a fashion, and quickly went out the door, grateful that the detective bureau was only ten minutes away.

On the front of his truck, standing there like some sort of hood ornament, he found the large glass of milk Ruth had left for him knowing he would not think to get it for himself. Skinny picked up the milk, looked around hopefully for a roll, discovered the jelly doughnut on the seat, and set out for the detective bureau office, happily finishing his breakfast before he had gone a block and a half. At the office, there well before shift change, he rearranged the papers on his desk and put a fresh cup of coffee near them. Then he called Mike Theriot, told him exactly what to do, and slipped back out, confident that he was covered for the hour or so he needed. At home, he shaved then showered and was wandering around his apartment, in his shorts, brushing his teeth, when he heard a knock at his door. Thinking it was Mike Theriot arriving, for Mike Theriot, amazingly fast, he yelled, "Come in," rather aggressively, spraying toothpaste foam out three feet in front of him.

The man who opened the door was about fifty years old. Inside his neatly pressed blue seersucker jacket, his shoulders were thin and stooped. His hair was thin and dark blond, parted on the side. He wore glasses with brown frames, and behind the clear, round lenses, his eyes were bright blue.

"My name is William Dryden," the man said, his voice surprisingly crisp. "I'm a special agent with the Drug Enforcement Administration."

Skinny thought that over for a moment, rubbing his hand over his stomach, hiding his surprise. To him, the guy looked more like a college teacher than a special agent from the DEA.

"Yeah?" he said. "So?"

"So as soon as you get your pants on," the special agent replied, "I'd like a few minutes of your time."

"Is this about what happened yesterday?" Skinny asked.

"Yes, it is," the special agent replied.

Skinny tapped his toothbrush against the open palm of his hand.

"I figured there were drugs involved somewhere."

Skinny moved to his left, into the kitchen, and bent at the waist to rinse out his mouth at the sink. When he looked up, across the counter that separated the small kitchen from the living room, he saw William Dryden near the far wall, studying the framed picture of his boat, the *No Special Hurry*, on its trailer, still wet from Bayou Barataria.

"That's Skinny's boat," Skinny explained. "Skinny goes fishing."

The special agent seemed to consider Skinny's comment, but he did not reply to it in any way at all. He looked from the picture to Skinny, then he looked around, saw the armchair across from the couch, and took a seat. He crossed his legs, revealing black socks, and composed his hands in his lap.

Skinny moved out from behind the counter and leaned against the wall, his arms crossed on his chest, just waiting.

"Do you want to put on your pants?" the special agent asked.

"I don't need pants to talk," Skinny replied. "I'm in a hurry," he added, as if that explained that.

The special agent made a mildly questioning face as he tried to put the two statements together.

"According to the report I saw," he began after a moment, "yesterday was your day off. You and your"—he paused, searching for the right word—"companion went down to Catfish Bend to collect driftwood. You saw a metal boat explode. You swam out to the boat, found the captain dead, and rescued a young boy." William Dryden looked up, looking for affirmation, and Skinny nodded. "The captain of the boat was named Evans Charles," he went on, his tone explanatory. "Evans Charles worked for a man who calls himself Ishanti—that's a new name for him. The name he had until a few years ago was Jerome Patterson."

Big Jerome, Skinny said to himself. Although it had been a few years since he had seen him, he knew him.

"Since being released from prison, Jerome—Ishanti—

has done pretty well for himself. He owns three clubs that we're certain about, and there are two or three others we suspect."

"What kind of clubs?" Skinny asked, genuinely curious.

"The Silver Lily is one of them," William Dryden replied. "I understand you went there to use the phone."

Skinny nodded again.

"You think Evans Charles was running drugs for this guy, Ishanti?"

"That's a possibility," William Dryden allowed, apparently distracted, looking off more than down. After a moment, he removed his glasses and rubbed the oval red spots on the bridge of his nose.

"And Ishanti was distributing the drugs through his clubs," Skinny went on, speculating out loud. "That sounds pretty likely. Something went sour, and Ishanti blew up the boat."

"That's the slant we're taking on it," William Dryden said. Without the shiny lenses in front of them, his eyes seemed somehow naked. He put his glasses back on. "The point I'm here to make is, we're already working the case—"

"What about the follow-up?" Skinny interrupted him. "What about the boy? He's still missing, right?"

"We're working that as well," William Dryden replied. He looked right at Skinny. "We'll find him."

Skinny pushed himself away from the wall, annoyed that someone else was about to tell him to stay off the case. It wasn't his problem anyway: all he wanted was for the boy to be found so that Ruth would get back to normal.

"As far as I'm concerned, whoever finds the boy gets the witness," he said matter-of-factly, not acceding at all. "Whoever has the witness makes the case."

For a long moment, William Dryden did not say anything, but his eyes took on a searching, uncertain quality,
as if he had something to say but could not quite find the
words to convey it.

"The boy is the first priority," he agreed finally. He
rested his elbows on the arms of the chair and interlaced
his fingers in front of his face, looking over them, then
at Skinny. "We have a man in place. Anything you do on
your own places him at risk." He dropped his arms to the
arms of the chair. "That's not information I normally like
to give out."

Skinny thought about that for a moment, unconvinced—and reasonably unconcerned. Maybe the guy did
have someone next to Ishanti. If so, in one way he was
right: if he just left him in place, anything Skinny did
created risk. But maybe he didn't have anyone. Maybe
he just wanted to beat out the guy from the ATF. Either
way, it wasn't Skinny's concern: he wasn't going to go after
the boy directly, but he wasn't going to *not* go after him
either, for two reasons. First, he felt some responsibility—
he had, after all, rescued the boy and turned him over to
his aunt. Second, if he just let it go, Ruth would shoot him.

"What about the boat that blew up?" he asked. "Have
you found out who owned it?"

William Dryden did not seem inclined to answer the
question. He looked at Skinny with eyes that were assessing, no longer uncertain—and not very patient.

"I received a second report last night," he said, a thin
edge on his words. "You were followed when you left
the Silver Lily Club: two men followed you as far as the
bridge."

"Too bad they turned off," Skinny interjected, not surprised that he had been in touch with Gatzke. "Skinny
knew right where to take 'em."

"You followed procedure," William Dryden went on. He stood up and moved close to Skinny, close enough that Skinny could smell the pipe-tobacco smoke in his clothes. "You made three right turns when you first spotted them."

"Yeah?" Skinny said. "So?" he added, though he knew exactly what he was saying: his man was one of the men in the car. That was the only way he could know about the three right turns he had made.

William Dryden just looked at him, then he moved away to the door. He glanced back, about to leave but ready to say something before he did; and just then the door opened and Mike Theriot walked in. William Dryden nodded curtly to Mike Theriot, moved around him and left, leaving the door open.

"Who was that?" Mike Theriot asked, coming on in.

"Skinny's not sure," Skinny replied vaguely, still affected by the look William Dryden had given him, his blue eyes icy cold, hard and shiny as the round lenses in front of them. "But Skinny'll say this," he added, wiping his hand across his face, "he's sure not a college professor."

After he had gotten in the van in the parking lot, Special Agent William Dryden stared out the windshield, looking up at Skinny's second-floor apartment, momentarily collecting his thoughts before he turned to the black man sitting in back.

The black man still had on the rust-red suit and white shirt he had worn to the Silver Lily Club the night before, when he had seen Skinny come in to use the phone.

"I told him we have a man in place," William Dryden said.

The black man glanced out the side window of the van, knowing the glass was mirrored and knowing he could not be seen. Sitting at the small, built-in table, he seemed even larger than he was.

"Do you think he'll stay away?" he asked.

William Dryden shrugged.

"As far as he's concerned, the boy is up for grabs."

The black man sat back in the bench-type seat and tried to put his feet up on the seat on the other side of the table, but his legs were too long.

"He's right about that," he remarked. "He is."

William Dryden glanced over his shoulder, out the windshield, then back into the van.

"Are you sure he knows Ishanti?" he asked.

"I'm sure," the black man replied. "When I was in the prison, I saw them together, him and Ishanti—except then Ishanti didn't have his clubs. He was still called Big Jerome."

"Big Jerome," William Dryden repeated, allowing the name to sink in, putting it together with what else he had learned.

"We'll see what he does," he said, gesturing back at Skinny's apartment, then turning around to start up the van.

"We'll see, all right," the black man agreed.

11

Dwayne was exhausted, so tired even his fear had begun to recede. He had tried to sleep on the batture, in the tall weeds near the foot of the levee, but it was cold and there were bugs and he had seen and heard things in the shadows once the bright lights had gone off. Before that, he had heard the men searching for him, calling his name. He had kept very still, hardly breathing, curled up behind a big driftwood log—one man had passed so close he could have reached out and grabbed his ankle.

He got to his knees and looked around in the fast-coming light. He knew he could not just stay where he was—someone would see him for sure—but he did not know what to do. In the distance, extended out into the low fog on the river, he could see his auntee's shack. It looked very quiet, quiet and peaceful, like it was floating. It made him think of his cot, of waking beneath the rough, green blanket his auntee always gave him, of the breakfast she would have made him on the hot plate, grits and eggs, probably, or grits and toast. He knew something bad had happened.

Dwayne got to his feet and ran, sprinting downriver away from the shack, his fear and sorrow wanting physical release. His oversize, high-topped sneakers flopped out in front of him. After a while, he got tired. Breathing hard, he slowed to a walk, trying to think what he should do, trying to remember.

After the white people had brought him back, he had gone with his auntee to her house; but they had only been there a minute, long enough to start up the generator and to get the lights going, when they had seen the boat coming up to the pier, drifting up fast, like it had been waiting for them, waiting in the clump of willow trees that were a little ways away, down in the water. His auntee had grabbed his hand hard and pulled him inside.

"You go out the back, boy," she had ordered him, holding to his hand even after he had tried to pull it away. "Shimmy down the posts like you do. You hide in the weeds until I call you."

He had done what she had ordered because something in her voice and the strength of her grip had frightened him. It had made a chill run up his spine. And as fast as he was, racing out the back door, scrambling over the side of the pier, using the cross braces between the pilings like the rungs on a jungle gym to drop himself down to the water's edge, he was just barely away when he heard the voices, loud and angry, first his auntee's then somebody else's, a man's, maybe a white man's, though he hadn't been sure, not with the generator making its racket. He had heard the gunshots, though, he *was* sure about that—he had heard gunshots before, more than once, over in the project, and the time his daddy had showed him how to shoot. After that, he had seen the white woman come up. Behind her, the skinny white man had come up, too, carrying a can that looked like gasoline.

What they doing here? Dwayne had asked himself. *Where he going with that gasoline?*

His foot snagged a half-buried piece of wire cable, and he tripped. Nearby, he saw a large cardboard box lying on its side. He crawled over to it and went on inside. He sat cross-legged, away from the open end, feeling secure just for the moment.

All his life, it seemed, people had left him. His mother had left so long before he couldn't even remember what she looked like. His grandmother had left, too, when he was living with her, dead one evening, day after that put away in a box. His father, he had left and come back, left and come back, trying to make a living, he said, trying to make money, him and Ishanti.

"Don't never trust Ishanti," his father had told him. "Take his money, but don't never trust him."

Now his father was gone and his auntee, too.

Left, he told himself. *Not coming back.* He felt his eyes begin to burn. *Shouldn't have listened.* He wiped at his eyes with the sleeve of his T-shirt. *Shouldn't have run off like I did.*

He looked down at the grains of brown river sand that had stuck to his sneakers.

"It don't mean nothing," he said out loud, his voice low. "Been left before. Don't matter."

"Don't matter," he repeated, using the words as he always did, using them to make his sadness into a steely, cold hardness.

He liked that, liked the way it felt to be hard and uncaring. Then the anger didn't hurt him. It made him feel strong. It made him want to hurt someone else, make *them* pay.

Suddenly, he thought of the box his daddy kept buried, near where he usually hid his boat. He thought of what was in it and knew exactly what to do first.

Upriver about a mile, behind another old pier, there was a pondlike backwater where the river ran over a sand bar and came in close to the levee. Trees grew at the water's edge—when the river was unusually high, they were right in the water—and behind that pier, in among the trees, was the overgrown spot Dwayne's father had used for a berth. Dwayne went back the way he had just run, then crossed the levee to go wide around his auntee's old shack. He recrossed the levee as soon as he thought it was safe and thereafter stayed on the batture, walking upriver.

Dwayne knew that stretch of the batture. He had gone that way often and had already examined most of the more interesting flotsam. He knew where to go to catch catfish and where it was safe to venture out into the water; so he was able to go straight to the old pier, even though from all sides it was completely hidden from view.

A narrow path led through the trees and around the water, bringing him to the foot of the walkway that went up to the pier. Rather than go up the walkway, however, he used it for reference and went past it, back into the trees. He found the railroad crosstie, then the old concrete-filled tire, and ten steps from that he dropped to his knees and began to dig, scooping the sand away from the box.

The box was an old crate that had been made to hold engine parts—Dwayne's father had found it on board the boat. Over the years, the wood had been darkened with grease and worn smooth by use. There were smears of green paint on it from when Dwayne and his father had painted the boat. When Dwayne had the sand scooped well away from it, he lifted the top off and put it to one side, looking inside the box with some anticipation, concerned that his father might somehow have changed things, then pleased when he saw that he hadn't. Carefully, as if they were fragile, he took out the guns, five of them in all, three revolvers and two pistols, and placed them side by side on the box's flat wooden top. Carelessly, he removed the inch-think sheaf of money, all old twenties and tens; then he reached back inside for the bullets. When the box was completely empty, Dwayne sat back and one at a time picked up each gun, examining it carefully before he aimed it, picturing vague faces and chests, making soft noises as if he were shooting.

"*Coosh*" was the sound he made. "*Coosh. Coosh.*"

It made him feel good to hold the guns. It made him feel the same steely hardness he had felt earlier. The guns gave possibility to his unfocused desire to strike back at his hurt, to strike out.

"Don't matter," he said as he tried to decide which gun to take.

He finally settled on the small five-shot revolver his father had showed him how to shoot. He divided up the money and took half of it. Before he tucked the revolver into his waistband, he checked to see that it was loaded and put extra bullets in his pocket—and it was then that he found the phone number Ruth had given him, the scrap of paper on which she had written her number.

Dwayne made sure everything else was back in the box before he set the top in place and reburied it, his face intensely determined as he patted down the sand.

12

Ruth was having trouble concentrating, which was unusual for her. As a rule, when she went to work she could put everything but the tasks immediately at hand out of her mind; but this morning was different: as hard as she tried, she could not keep herself focused. She kept replaying the events of the day and the night before, and she kept thinking about Dwayne, which she knew was both a very real concern about him and, she felt fairly certain, her way of externalizing her own questions about children.

She took a cigarette from the pack on her desk, automatically picked up her lighter, and lit it, momentarily forgetful that her office was a no-smoking area.

Across the room, a woman gave her a pained sidelong look that quickly made her remember.

Ruth stood up from her desk and went out into the hall, resentful of having to do so—and irritated with herself, irritated that she was worrying about something over which she had no control.

The hall outside the office led to a mezzanine, a wide gallery that overlooked the main floor of a bank. Forty feet below, men and women were coming and going, moving with purpose. Ruth could hear the muted hum of conversation and the sound of heels clicking on the highly polished stone floor. She leaned back against the heavy brass railing, looking in, back down the hallway that led to her office.

When Ruth thought of children, she felt an immediate ambivalence, a vacillating uncertainty she did not know how to resolve. On the one hand, she had what she felt were the normal urges and images, the desire to have a child all her own, the feeling a sleepy-headed little boy or girl would give her when he or she reached up to hug her good night. But as soon as those feelings formed, other things came to mind, hints of realities that were not quite so warm. Thinking practically, where, for instance, would she send a child to school? New Orleans's public schools were inner-city war zones, and even if she accepted the idea of private schools—which was, for her, a pretty big even if—she wasn't at all sure she could afford them.

"You just have to plunge on in, Ruth," her mother had told her, "and do what you have to. Somehow, you get by."

But Ruth wasn't about to just *plunge on in* to motherhood. She wasn't twenty years old anymore and unaware of consequences.

"You're just being selfish," her mother had added.

"That's too simple," Ruth had replied, stung by her mother's comment, "and very likely untrue."

Sure, she admitted readily, she wanted things for herself. She didn't want just to "get by." She wanted to go to the movies when she pleased and to buy clothes when the urge struck her. Someday, she even wanted a new car, not a used one—she had been working for twenty years, and she had earned it. But that wasn't it, not in itself, she knew that for certain.

Ruth wrapped one arm across her middle and laid her other arm on top of it, holding her cigarette well away from her blouse.

Things had changed, she thought, since her mother had had her. It's not like it once was, when more people were needed, when it was okay just to follow your instincts. There were enough people now, God knew, enough social problems, enough valid reasons not to have children to make the real question, Why? Why have them? Not, why not?—something she could not hope to explain to her mother in a hundred years trying. Of the couples she knew who had children most had done so for themselves, not for the child. They made the child the relentless center of attention, a distraction from everything else, a shield. That was why, she believed, "parenting" had become such a popular expression: it implied an activity, like sailing or bowling, whereas "being a parent" defined a station in life.

So what about Dwayne? she asked herself. *Why is he so important?*

That's the sixty-four-dollar question, she answered herself, because, obviously, she could not have become so attached to him in such a short period of time. What she was confronting, what was creating such emotional content, she knew, was her uncertainty and the fact that, if she did not have children fairly soon, she would not be able to have them at all, the ramifications of which she did not have time to consider because a woman from her office stuck her head out the door to tell her that she had a call.

"He's on hold on line three," the woman said. Her face softened, expressing a mild uncertainty. "It sounds like a little boy."

Ruth hurried down the hall and into her office, grabbing the phone at the desk nearest the door.

"This is Ruth," she said, feeling a quick panic when there was no immediate response. "Dwayne? Dwayne, is that you?" The line hummed. "Are you there?"

"Didn't know who else to call," Dwayne said finally, his voice sullen. "Found the number you gave me. Called you."

"You did exactly right," Ruth replied, trying to reassure him; then she forced herself to make her voice easy. "I'm really glad that you called."

"Spent the night on the batture," Dwayne continued.

My God, Ruth said to herself.

The woman at the desk glanced up long enough to give Ruth an annoyed look, obviously irritated that she was using her phone.

Ruth turned her back.

"I'll come get you. Where are you?"

"Saw you come over the levee last night," Dwayne went on, not answering the question, "you and your boyfriend, him carrying that gasoline." There was an accusation in his tone, an accusation with just the trace of a question.

"We thought the generator was running out of gas, Dwayne. We wanted to help—I'd like to help now."

For a while Dwayne did not say anything, then he asked, "Is my auntee dead?"

"Yes," Ruth replied, searching for the clear strength

she had felt earlier when she had watched Dwayne asleep on her bed. "Yes, she is."

"Thought so," Dwayne said, then he was silent again.

Ruth did not know what to say, so she just held on, looking around the office without really seeing, trying to check her emotions.

"When I on your bed," Dwayne said finally, "I not really asleep, just pretending."

"I sort of suspected that," Ruth replied.

"When you went on outside, I got up, looked out the front window. Seen the man drive up, seen you talking with him."

On Dwayne's end of the line, a loud noise intruded, probably a truck.

"Seen him before, with my daddy."

"Who?" Ruth asked, not following, straining to hear. "Who had you seen before? The policeman?"

There was a hesitant quality to Dwayne's silence this time, a thoughtfulness, as if he were puzzling things out.

"I didn't think he was a policeman, either," Ruth explained, sensing his question, "since he wasn't wearing a uniform. But he's from an office called Alcohol, Tobacco, and Firearms—that's a branch of the government. They investigate explosions, like the one on the boat."

Dwayne seemed to think that over as well.

"My daddy dead, too," he said finally.

"I know," Ruth replied softly.

"Don't matter."

"Of course it matters—"

"I come by your house," Dwayne interrupted, his tone surprisingly forceful. "Come by later, soon as I can."

"I can pick you up, Dwayne," Ruth offered.

"I get there myself," Dwayne replied.

Ruth considered the situation, then conceded.

"I'll be there. I'll wait for you."

"You be there by yourself," Dwayne added, his tone now more than forceful, almost tough. "Don't want to see no police."

Ruth thought about that for a moment, wondering why he was concerned about the police, but by the time both answers came to her, Dwayne had already hung up the phone.

13

When Ruth was put through on the radio, Skinny and Mike Theriot were working a drive-by shooting during which multiple shots had been fired, though as near as they could tell, no one had been hit by any bullets. They had been in the area, less than two blocks away, when the call had come out as shots fired, and at Skinny's insistence they had rolled, Theriot driving, going, it seemed to Skinny, about the same speed as he went to the grocery.

"For Christ's sake," Skinny had said, watching the pavement move past at something less than a blur. "I can walk faster than this."

"It's those long legs," Mike Theriot agreed smugly, glad that Skinny was *not* doing the driving. It wasn't their call, after all, and technically they shouldn't even be responding.

Arriving at the scene sometime thereafter, they had found one man down in the middle of the street, a car up on the sidewalk, and a crowd of spectators already assembled. After a call for an ambulance and a quick couple of questions, they had determined that a car coming upon the drive-by car had swerved to avoid the spray of bullets, causing the driver of the drive-by car to swerve in return and thereby to run over the pedestrian he had actually been trying to shoot—the car on the sidewalk just happened to be parked there.

Uniformed officers arrived and with Skinny's help asked another few questions.

The perpetrator, it seemed, appeared to be somewhere between five four and six eight, depending upon whom they asked. He was wearing either a faded black shirt or a bright red one, though it might have been green. The suspect vehicle was either a Ford, a Toyota, or some kind of a truck.

"Jesus Christ," Skinny said to the most reluctant of the witnesses, "the guy opens up out his window with a machine gun then runs over your cousin, and you're worried about talking to *me*? I'd worry about *him*."

"Ain't going to be no snitch," the young man replied.

Skinny gave him a hard look, then shook his head.

"Jesus Christ," he said again, and walked over to the uniformed officer who was waving at him, not in his best possible humor.

"Say, Skinny," the officer said, "maybe you can settle something for us."

The two uniformed officers who had responded to the call were standing about seven feet apart, at the head and the foot of the man down in the street. Skinny knew one of the officers—the one who had waved at him—but he did not know the other.

"See how he's lying?" the officer started. "With the yellow line beneath his neck?"

Skinny looked at the man down and saw that he was, indeed, on top of the line that divided the street. Although the man had been bounced around considerably and had obviously broken his nose, he did not seem in immediate peril. Every once in a while he gave out a moan, hawked up the blood in his throat, and spat it out, mumbling as he did so about some about-to-be-dead motherfucker. Skinny watched him spit once, then looked away.

"So here's the question," the officer went on. "This side of the line"—he pointed down, at his feet—"this is my beat. That side of the line"—he pointed at the other officer—"that's his beat."

"Yeah?" Skinny remarked. "So?"

"So if this guy quits breathing, who has to give him artificial respiration? His head's not in my beat, so it's not my responsibility, right?"

"But his chest *is* in your beat," the other officer argued, "and that's where he needs the air. In his chest."

They can't be serious was Skinny's first thought. *This is some kind of a joke.*

But he looked again at the man, saw the blood dribbling from his discolored lips, more blood coming down from his nose, and realized he wouldn't, himself, be too keen about even clearing the airway, much less about putting his mouth there.

"For Christ's sake," he said for want of an answer, and it was just after that that Mike Theriot came up and, without telling him who it was, handed him the radio.

When Ruth heard Skinny say, "What?" his voice loud and nasal, hollow sounding in the relayed connection, for a moment she questioned why she had called him. She knew, of course, that he would want to know about Dwayne's call, but as far as she was concerned, her meeting with him was her business. Her course was set. Dwayne, she had realized, did not want the police around for two very good reasons: first, if his father had been involved in something illegal, which seemed very probable, then likely he considered himself guilty of that something as well; and second, it was likely, too, that he already knew about the youth homes, about how he could be taken in whether or not he had committed a crime.

But this is Skinny, she chided herself, *not the police*, a distinction at that moment she found it disturbingly difficult to make.

"Dwayne called," she said, hearing her words echo down the line, as if she were calling someplace distant.

"You aren't going to believe this one," Skinny said when he heard who it was, referring to his present situation. "So what did he say?" he added.

"He said he spent the night on the batture," Ruth replied. She took a paper clip from the magnetic holder on her desk and unbent it, straightening out the malleable metal. "He wanted to know what had happened to his aunt."

"What did you tell him?"

"I told him she was dead."

"Good," Skinny remarked. "When in doubt, tell the truth. Did he say where he was?"

"He wouldn't tell me," Ruth replied. She wrapped the paper clip around her first finger. "I'm going to meet him."

"Where?"

"He asked me not to say, Skinny. He asked me to be alone."

Skinny seemed to consider that, then he said, "Wait," rather tersely. "The ambulance just got here," he explained. In the background Ruth heard him yell, "Theriot. Make sure that guy is still breathing."

For about a half minute thereafter, Skinny apparently put his hand over the mouthpiece, and Ruth heard nothing else.

"Thank Christ," he said just before he came back on the line. "Sorry," he said when he did.

"Dwayne was looking out the front window when we thought he was asleep," Ruth went on, trying to move past the fact that she was going to meet him alone. "He said that he had seen Gatzke before."

"I already figured that," Skinny replied, his words edged with impatience. "I figured Gatzke was working a case against Dwayne's father—I told you." Before Ruth could say anything else, he went right to the point she had tried to avoid. "So you're not going to tell me where he is?"

"I don't know where he is, Skinny," she hedged.

"Where you're going to meet him then, for Christ's sake."

Ruth did not say anything to that—she did not know quite what *to* say—and in the uneasy silence that followed she tightened the wire around her finger and watched as her fingertip turned dark red, then purple, the ridges and swirls standing out in relief. She knew Skinny was going to be angry with her, and she knew, too, that in a way he had a right to be; but when she thought of Dwayne and of all that had happened to him, of where he was now, alone, out on the street, with no one to trust and nowhere to turn, his anger paled.

"There's no point to this," she said finally.

"Skinny'll buy *that*," Skinny snapped, his anger evident.

"He needs someone to trust, Skinny. Look what he's been through. He's a little boy. He's frightened."

"It's dangerous for you to go alone, Ruth. I wouldn't even go by myself. Someone is after him—"

"I don't think it's too much to ask—"

"Someone," Skinny overrode her, his tone emphatic, "who has killed two people already. It's a dangerous situation. It *is* too much to ask."

Skinny allowed time for his words to sink in, and Ruth let them hang, knowing the burden of the silence was hers.

"So we disagree," she said finally.

"Jesus Christ," Skinny replied.

"I'll call you as soon as I can," Ruth went on, "when I'm with him."

"You do what you have to, Ruth," Skinny said, his anger just as evident but mixed now with frustration.

Ruth felt bad about the whole conversation. She knew she was being maddeningly stubborn, maybe even acting unwisely, but she knew, too, that she could make it up to Skinny, which was not something she could say about Dwayne.

"Are you still at your office?" Skinny asked.

"Yes," Ruth replied.

"Then you call me when you're getting ready to leave, and you call me as soon as you have him."

"I will," Ruth agreed readily. "And I'll be careful, Skinny. I promise. Miss Chicken Little, you know me."

There was a long pause before Skinny said, "Maybe not as well as I thought."

14

Mike Theriot had to break into a run to catch up to Skinny. When he caught up, he slowed to a fast walk and said, "I got hold of two guys in Intelligence who owe me a favor. They'll be outside Ruth's office in five minutes." He glanced at his watch. "Seven minutes tops."

Skinny acknowledged that with a nod, his pace steady, his lips pressed tightly together.

After Skinny had yelled to Mike Theriot to make sure the man down was still breathing, in the moment Theriot had hesitated, wondering why he should check since the paramedics were already at work, Skinny had waved him over and told him what was happening.

"The boy called Ruth." As he had spoken, Skinny had held the radio in front of his chest, his palm flattened over the microphone. "She wants to go by herself to meet him."

In the late morning sun, his eyes were bright green, bright green flecked with yellow.

"I'm pretty sure she's still at her office. Get somebody over there. Now. Make sure it's an unmarked unit, and make sure they know what she looks like. She parks in the lot at St. Charles and Common. She'll take her car. The lot's on a corner. There are two ways out."

"Are you sure—?" Mike Theriot had begun, a little skeptical because he knew Skinny and he knew Ruth and he knew which of the two was more impulsive.

"I'm sure," Skinny had said, and his dead-serious look had convinced him.

"Last I saw, the guy *was* still breathing," Mike Theriot had noted before he had moved away to get on his radio.

"Thank Christ," Skinny had said just before he had started in again with Ruth.

At the car, Skinny went around to the driver's side and got in behind the wheel.

Mike Theriot got in and buckled his seat belt.

Ruth unclenched her fist, took the paper clip off her finger, and dropped it into the trash can beneath her desk. She heard the bent wire hit the trash can's metal bottom, and she felt a twinge of guilt: the empty sound made her realize she had not done any work at all. Her desk looked exactly the same as when she had gotten there that morning.

She glanced around, saw no one was paying any attention to her, glanced at her watch, trying not to think about Skinny, trying to decompress. In a few minutes she planned to leave early for lunch, and after that she intended to call in to say she was not coming back. She would go to her car and go home to wait for Dwayne, and the more she thought about it, the more convinced she became that that was hardly too much for Dwayne to ask.

Look what he's been through, she said to herself and began to rearrange the papers on her desk. *Skinny's just being Skinny.*

An overdue report caught her eye. She had promised to have it typed by that afternoon.

"Damn," she said softly and took it off the stack of other work in progress, wondering what she should do. Quickly, she took the report to another woman in the office, explained what had to be done, went back to her desk. Satisfied that her other work could wait and anxious to be moving, she took her purse from the drawer where she kept it, put the long strap over her shoulder, and left, calling out that she would be back in an hour.

On the mezzanine Ruth lit a cigarette then put it out, unsmoked, when the elevator arrived. She cut across the main floor of the bank, to the side entrance, and went outside, fumbling through her purse as she did so, looking for her parking lot ticket, trying to avoid the early lunch crowd, not at all put off when two men started to pass her, one on each side.

At the same time, as if there had been some sort of signal, each of the men took one of her elbows and simply steered her, using her own forward momentum but hurrying her pace, turning her, walking her down the alley that ran alongside the bank.

Ruth was so unprepared for the move that she went several steps before it even occurred to her to be alarmed. She tried to slow down, but the two men kept moving her forward.

"Scream," she heard in her ear, the voice low but emphatic, full of venom, "and I break your fucking neck."

Ruth was surprised by how unafraid she felt, how calm inside.

The man on her right was shorter than she was, short and stocky, heavily built. He moved with short, pistonlike strides. The man on her left was a monster, a full head taller than she was and at least twice as broad. She could feel the solid mass of him just in the way he held her, his huge hand wrapped completely around her upper arm, his massive shoulder forcing her on, as if the side of a house had rolled up behind her.

Down the alley about twenty yards, there was a large blue dumpster, and behind that there was an alcove, the recessed opening of a bricked-over doorway.

The monster moved her into the opening and spun her around, standing so close in front of her all she could see was his face. The skin on his cheeks was purple-black and smooth, made even darker by black razor stubble. His eyes were flat black and angry.

Ruth felt the fear begin in her legs, a deep quivering tremor.

"Where's the boy?" the monster asked, and before she could answer—before she could even think to answer— he slapped her.

The stinging-thudding pain centered on her ear.

"Where's the boy?" he asked again.

The second slap came just as quickly.

Ruth felt a trickle of blood seep from her nose. She felt his hand at her throat.

"I've got all day," the man said, the pressure on her throat increasing, making it difficult to breath. "I'm about to ask you again."

Panic took hold of her and Ruth flailed, grabbing the man's arm and trying to move it, hitting it, raking it with her nails.

He hit her again, harder.

"Where's the boy?" he said, unaffected.

When her head cleared, Ruth knew then that she was going to die. He was going to kill her. She was sure of it. She knew it, and with the certainty came a shift, a clear anger and quick, powerful images, of Skinny, of how displeased he would be, of his expression when he heard; of her apartment, quiet on a late summer afternoon, sunlight streaming in through the windows, heavy and thick enough to cut with a knife; of Dwayne, just out of the river, wet and starting to shiver, looking so troubled and alone.

"You bastard," she said to the man, feeling the blood in her mouth, seeing some of it spray.

It was hard to tell, but the man did not seem to take that personally. He did not seem to get any angrier. There were more questions and more blows, but thereafter it seemed to Ruth that she was going away inside herself, someplace where he couldn't touch her, someplace warm and dark and very, very comfortable, someplace where no answers were needed.

15

Skinny saw Ruth's car, right in the lot where he had expected it to be, and across the street he saw Theriot's two friends from Intelligence staking it out; but after a deliberately slow trip around the block, still he had not seen Ruth, so he decided to find a pay phone to call her at her office, to see whether or not she was there. At the corner he saw two things at once: a pay phone and a small crowd gathering on the sidewalk farther up the block. He pulled to the curb, got out at the phone, sent Theriot to see what was happening. As he fished in his pocket for change and dialed Ruth's number, he watched Theriot go on down the street, get out of the car, step into the crowd. Just as the phone answered, he saw Theriot emerge from the crowd and wave at him frantically, motioning for him to come up where he was.

Skinny left the phone hanging. He took one long step then another, increasing the pace of his overlong strides, finally breaking into a run, feeling his heart in his chest, knowing, just knowing it was Ruth.

The crowd was very different from the one Skinny and Mike Theriot had left at the scene of the drive-by shooting. These people wore coats and ties and fashionable dresses and stood quietly, talking in whispers, looking concerned and a bit guilty, knowing they were doing no good whatsoever, knowing they should move on. They moved out of the way, stepping back, clearing a path, when they saw Skinny coming.

Ruth had almost made it out of the alley. Not really conscious, moving on survival instinct alone, she had crawled from behind the dumpster, back toward the sidewalk, and had collapsed about ten yards in from the street. Her knuckles were red and raw from clutching her purse as she crawled. Her knees were black and filthy. Around her throat were the first darkening signs of the bruises that were coming. The front of her dress and the lower half of her face were covered with blood.

Skinny dropped down beside her, put his ear on her chest, heard her heartbeat, reassuringly strong. Quickly he checked for broken bones, found none apparent, examined her eyes, using his thumbs to pull back the eyelids. He glanced down the alley then back toward the street, noting the distances, knowing without reconstructing it what had happened. He nodded to Mike Theriot, slipped his arms under Ruth's legs and the back of her neck, and stood up with her, remaining motionless for a moment, getting his balance. He saw that, as he had lifted her, the front of Ruth's dress had pulled open, and he said to Mike Theriot, "Fix that, will you?" his voice very low.

Mike Theriot closed up the dress, then moved on ahead, getting the crowd out of the way, using gestures and language a bit rougher than were actually needed.

Mike Theriot opened the door of the car, and Skinny laid Ruth on the backseat then squatted down on the floor beside her. He took Ruth's hand in his own. He heard the car doors close and Mike Theriot on the radio. He heard the siren, the squeal of the tires, the horn. He was aware of all that was happening around him, but just then the sounds seemed to come from very far away.

16

Ruth heard a snap and felt a sharp stinging sensation that briefly intruded on the comfortable blackness; and after that, though she was somehow aware that it was of her own making, she had the most lucid, most pleasant dream that she'd ever had: in her mind, she renovated her apartment, making a bedroom for Dwayne. She took out one wall, put two in its place, added a door, imagining each step of the process. She saw the old wall coming out, the new walls framing in, the new wiring and the sheetrock. She smelled the fresh paint and the carpet. She saw the deliverymen bringing in the new furniture, the bed, the mattress, the low chest of drawers with a mirror. When the room was complete, when she'd hung the curtains herself and straightened the bedspread, she decided to redo it again, to make sure that she'd gotten it just right. She felt a happiness, a satisfaction, a glad anticipation she had never known, though it came to her gradually, as the painkiller wore off and pain came in its place, that at least some of her feelings had been drug-induced.

Suddenly, she was extraordinarily thirsty. She opened

her eyes slightly, saw a straw right at her lips, took it, and sucked on it greedily.

"Sip it," she heard someone say, and she slowed down, savoring the cold, sweet liquid. When she had had enough, she opened her eyes and saw Skinny.

"You're a mess," he said, his expression at the same time both concerned and relieved.

Ruth tried to open her eyes further but realized her left eye wasn't working as it should. She tried to bring up her left hand to feel it but was restrained by the tube running into that arm; so with her right hand she touched her left cheek, probing the swelling. She felt the thick wad of tape across her nose.

"It's broken," Skinny explained.

"Terrific," Ruth remarked, her voice a croak. Under her hand she felt the control for the bed. She pressed a button, heard the motor hum quietly, found herself going up to a sitting position.

"The doctor said you're okay," Skinny went on, remembering the times he had been in the hospital himself, that those were the words he had most liked to hear—that and "No permanent damage."

"I don't feel okay," Ruth took exception.

"You don't look so good either," Skinny agreed. "Maybe next time you'll listen to Skinny."

Even with one eye swollen just about shut, Ruth gave him such a withering look that Skinny decided to note the other option as well.

"Maybe not," he added.

He shrugged.

"I called work for you. I told them that you'd been mugged."

Ruth was relieved to hear that, relieved that he hadn't gone into detail.

"What about Dwayne?" she asked.

Skinny shook his head.

"No word."

Ruth looked away, out the window, giving herself a moment to think past the thumping, dull pain, and was surprised to see that the sun was low, close to setting. The fall light was thin, very different from the thick light in summer, and she could almost feel the coolness outside, the lack of warmth, winter approaching. She had never liked the fall, she noted. She liked the summer. Even when New Orleans's heat and humidity had most people sweltering, she never complained—she knew those days were for her. She liked the heat and the life it brought, the summery clothes, the daily rains, the sense that everything was growing. She liked the way the sunlight seemed to penetrate right through to her bones. Fall made her feel life was slipping away, a feeling just then that brought with it immeasurable sadness. So much had happened. She thought of Dwayne, out on the street, more alone than ever, no doubt wondering what had happened to her, wondering why she hadn't shown up; and she thought of the man who had beaten her, the anger and hate in his face, the total lack of conscience. And for some reason she put one face in place of the other, momentarily seeing Dwayne full-grown, seeing the hate and anger in *his* eyes, realizing as soon as the image was formed that one *could* very easily become the other, that without help Dwayne *could* become such a monster.

"We have to find him, Skinny," she said. She felt tears well up in her eyes. "We have to."

"We're looking, Ruth," Skinny replied. "We're doing everything possible. We'll find him."

"I know," Ruth said quietly, looking around for a tissue, spotting the dispenser on the table beside the bed.

Skinny moved the tissues to the bed, within easy reach. Ruth took one and dabbed at her eyes.

"I was wondering," Skinny began tentatively, "are you sure it was Dwayne who called?" Ruth seemed puzzled by that, so he went on, "Could it have been someone who just sounded like Dwayne?"

"No," Ruth replied, considering the possibility, understanding what he was suggesting, that the call had been used to lure her out of her office. "No, it was Dwayne, I'm sure of it." She wadded up the tissue and held it in one hand. "I recognized the two men, Skinny," she explained, knowing he was questioning how someone had caught up to her and wanting him to see another possibility. "I'd seen them—we both saw them last night. They were behind us on the expressway."

"The two guys who followed us?" Skinny asked, his tone loud and incredulous. "The two black guys?"

Ruth nodded. She saw the color drain from Skinny's face.

"Jesus Christ," he said, obviously perturbed, running one hand through his hair, starting to step away but staying right where he was. "Jesus Christ," he said again.

Ruth did not say anything but looked at him, expecting him to explain why that was so unsettling.

"Describe them," he said, his voice terse, almost angry. "Describe them in detail."

Ruth did as he asked and described both men completely, though even as she did, it was apparent that Skinny was not really listening, not like he usually did, with his whole attention focused on every detail. He looked past her as she spoke, at the wall over her head, as if he were looking off at some point in the distance. When she finished, he nodded. He glanced at her, then looked off again and ran one hand over his face.

Ruth put her hand on the hand he kept on the bed rail.

After a while, Skinny looked at Ruth again, his eyes on her eyes.

"You scared the shit out of me," he said.

"I was scared myself," Ruth admitted. "I thought he was going to kill me." She felt her eyes start to burn. "At first I was frightened, then I got angry."

Skinny dropped down the rail on the bed and moved the box of tissues so that he could sit down beside her.

"I wanted to hurt him."

"I'll get you a gun, if you want."

"No," Ruth said, and shook her head. "No, I don't want a gun." She smiled wanly. "My purse is heavy enough as it is."

Ruth thought Skinny would smile at that, too, but he didn't; rather, he took her hand in both of his and looked at it closely, turning it over and back, examining the scrapes on her knuckles and on the heel of her hand. In his expression Ruth saw something she had never before seen, a frighteningly emotionless determination, a cold, controlled sort of anger.

"Skinny," she said firmly, "you don't have to hurt him." She took away her hand and indicated her face. "Not for this."

Skinny seemed to think that over for a moment, then he said, "I know I don't *have* to."

17

Skinny had always had to fight for what was his. That part of life didn't bother him a bit. From the time he had been thirteen years old, when the spurt of growth had left him skinny rather than just thin, in the neighborhood he had grown up in one lesson had been pounded into him repeatedly: back down half a step, give any ground whatsoever, and eventually someone will try to take what was rightfully yours—a little piece of personal understanding so much a part of him he hardly considered it as he waited outside 1001 Howard, the high-rise building that held the regional office of the DEA. A few minutes before, from a pay phone on the first floor of the hospital, he had called the DEA office and asked for Special Agent William Dryden. When the call was put through, he had hung up. He had gone outside, taken a taxi downtown, retrieved Ruth's car from the lot. He had driven to the thirty-story white building with black vertical stripes, considered where to park, and now was in the shadows away from the entrance, impatiently biding his time, pacing back and forth, stopping occasionally to gnaw at the side of his finger.

When William Dryden appeared, Skinny followed him, knowing exactly what he was going to do and waiting for the right opportunity. The sun had set quickly, and in the darkening twilight the man-made lights—the traffic signals, the headlights and the streetlights, the lights reflected on chrome—all seemed particularly clear and distinct. People seemed vague, dull in comparison.

Skinny was surprised at how fast the special agent walked, how much ground he covered with his apparently relaxed stride. He did not look around at all, which, Skinny knew, was a hazard of being accustomed to following someone else. When the special agent crossed Loyola, a wide six-lane thoroughfare, Skinny crossed also, flapping along behind him.

By the time he had gone another half block, it was apparent to Skinny where William Dryden was headed: he was going to the main post office to drop off the letters he was carrying, then more than likely he was heading to the government employees' parking garage right near there. So Skinny skipped on ahead, ducking past the post office to the garage. He positioned himself between the elevator and the ramp, in a small space reserved for motorcycles, where he could look out without being seen. When the special agent appeared and pushed the button for the elevator, Skinny stayed right where he was; but when the elevator doors began to open, in five overlong strides he was right behind him, not slowing down at all as he approached but seeming to walk right through him, using his momentum to slam the special agent into the stainless steel doors.

William Dryden hit hard and bounced.

"Oops," Skinny said and kept going. "Watch out," he added, and pushed William Dryden into the elevator itself, slamming him into a corner. He reached over the special agent's shoulder, grabbed his tie, looped it all the way around his neck, and held it tight as he reached back to press a button, his knee in the small of William Dryden's back, holding him pressed into the corner.

"What level you on?" Skinny asked, considering.

The special agent made a choking sound in reply.

Skinny shrugged and hit the button for the uppermost level.

"You fucked up," he said, though he was pretty sure the special agent was already getting the message.

The top floor of the parking garage was a huge concrete deck that sloped slightly toward the down ramp. Because it was both highest up and open to the weather, only one car was parked there, a car with an out-of-state plate that Skinny figured was probably stolen. The view of downtown was partially obstructed and not the best possible angle.

Skinny spun William Dryden out of the elevator and went out behind him, noting that, to his credit, the special agent kept his composure. Once he had regained his balance and loosened his tie, he adjusted his glasses, looking at Skinny as he did so, his blue eyes hard as glass and coldly inquiring.

"Who's your man?" Skinny asked, his voice loud and nasal, bending forward at the waist to give his question emphasis. "What's his name?"

William Dryden's eyes were steady on his.

"What are you talking about?" he asked evenly.

"Are you telling me you don't know? You saying that? You saying you don't know he beat the shit out of Ruth?" He stepped in close and poked the special agent in the chest. "*Your* man. She recognized him—the one you were so proud of this morning. The one who saw Skinny make three right turns."

William Dryden's gaze faltered, but just for a moment. "I didn't know," he said.

For a long moment Skinny kept his face right in William Dryden's, then he stood up straight.

"Jesus Christ," he said, for some reason believing him, believing something he had seen in his eyes.

Unaware that he was doing so, William Dryden brushed his thinning blond hair from his forehead, obviously thinking.

"How is she?" he asked. "Is she badly hurt?"

"Like you give a fuck, right?" Skinny snapped. He ran one hand through his hair, front to back. "She'll be okay," he said, reassuring himself more than William Dryden. "She's hurt, but she'll be okay."

The special agent accepted that without comment, knowing there was not much he could say, and Skinny seemed to hit an impasse himself, a flat spot in his thoughts; so they just stood there for a few moments, William Dryden groping for what should come next, Skinny trying to regain his focus.

Finally, William Dryden said, "Why didn't you tell me you knew Big Jerome?"

Skinny made a sour face and stared at him long enough to show that that wasn't what *he* had in mind.

"You never asked," Skinny replied, involuntarily thinking of Big Jerome, catching an image of him, remembering most of all the slablike size of his arms.

Before he had actually become a policeman, while awaiting the start of the next police academy, Skinny had worked in the parish prison. It was there that he had met Big Jerome. Big Jerome had taken charge of the black inmates, which, for all practical purposes, meant that he had run the place. Skinny had gone to him with various problems—about an inmate who had refused to leave his cell, about someone stopping up the guards' toilets, about a knife missing from the kitchen—and in short order all the problems had been solved. In return, Skinny had simply been straight with him, letting him know what he would and would not tolerate during his shift.

"No use we can't get along," Big Jerome had told him, explaining his ready cooperation. "We all locked in here together."

"Yeah," Skinny had replied confidently, pointing at his own chest, "but I have the key."

"You do," Big Jerome had laughed, heartily amused, about to give Skinny his first lesson about life in the prison, "'long as *I* let you keep it."

When Skinny had tried to leave the exercise yard, two inmates had rather casually blocked the way. When he had looked up at the guard tower, checking, just in case, he had seen the guard stationed there studiously looking the other way. If he thought about it enough, he could still feel the chill he had felt, the sudden cold, like a shadow across the crowded prison yard.

"Skinny'd get out, partner," he had called to Big Jerome. "He'd get out. Count on it. Then he'd come back."

Big Jerome had chuckled before he had waved Skinny out of the yard.

"And besides that," Skinny explained to William Dryden, "it's not like we were buddies." He put his hands in the side pockets of his jacket. "He ran the place. If you were in the prison, you knew Big Jerome. Ishanti," he corrected himself. "Whatever the shit he calls himself now."

William Dryden nodded slightly, and his eyes skipped around, from the pavement to the elevator to the car parked in the corner.

"I'm going to let my man stay loose," he said, his eyes coming back to Skinny, coming right to the point, his voice firm and decisive. "I'll yank his leash, but I'm not going to bring him in."

Skinny locked his eyes on the special agent's eyes.

"We're too close," William Dryden went on. "We've got too much invested to pull out now."

"You have to beat out the ATF, right?" Skinny's voice was very even, uncharacteristically flat, giving away the anger he was finding it hard to control. "They're working the case, too."

"I don't know what the ATF is doing," William Dryden replied coldly, immediately seeing what Skinny was saying and not at all liking it. "They don't consult with me about their investigations."

"But you hear things," Skinny kept on. "You hear things, and you put it together: they're working Ishanti, too, but they're coming at him from a different direction. They have a guy on the boat. You have a guy in his business. The boat gets sunk, their man is dead. So you're going to push now because you've got a clear shot." Skinny shrugged, a quick, tight movement of his shoulders. "I understand what's happening, partner." He looked right at William Dryden. "Why else would you let your man stay loose even when you're not sure what he's up to?"

William Dryden, unaffected, seemed to consider that, then he said, "There are other factors involved. You're not seeing the whole picture."

"Right," Skinny snapped. "I'm kind of short-sighted. All I see is two people dead, a boy out on the street, and Ruth having to eat through a straw." He flung one long arm out to the side.

"My man did not kill either of those two people,"

William Dryden said emphatically, his words spaced apart and distinct. "Either Evans Charles or Agnes Charles."

"You're pretty fucking certain of him," Skinny observed, "especially since you didn't know he had gotten to Ruth."

"I'm certain," William Dryden replied. "Certain enough *not* to bring him in."

Skinny took a step back and ran his hand over his face, then he stepped forward and grabbed William Dryden's tie, snapping it forward, jerking the special agent's face right into his face, wanting to see something in the man's eyes, something more than cool consideration, wanting him to feel the anger he felt.

The special agent tried to pull back, but Skinny held tight.

"If I were you," Skinny said, his words gaining emphasis from the controlled edge on his tone, "I'd bring him in anyway, no matter how certain I was." He pulled the tie even tighter. "I'd take him off the street before Skinny found him."

William Dryden held his gaze, but Skinny could see the effort it took. Behind the special agent's aggravation, there was concern, some doubt, and even a little spark of fear.

Skinny shoved William Dryden back, turned away, and started walking down from the roof, his overlong strides made even longer by the steep slope of the ramp.

18

There were several things Skinny wanted to do, but first among them was to check on Ruth, so from the parking garage he went back to the hospital. He found Ruth asleep, decided to stay awhile, settled himself in on the uncomfortable armchair beside the bed. It was quiet in the hospital, but in the quiet there was a subtle undercurrent of ongoing activity not too much different from the undercurrent of life in the prison: he could hear televisions turned low, people passing in the hall, the sounds of whispered conversations. Skinny wasn't really sleepy so he just sat there, thinking of Ruth, thinking of what she had come to mean to him, of how intertwined their lives had become.

Neither one of them was a kid anymore, that much was for certain, and Skinny realized he was just beginning to understand what that meant. For one thing, it meant that gratification was intermixed with long-term satisfaction, the always-present question of what to do was replaced more and more often by consideration of what could get done. The present was somehow less pressing, which was why, he supposed, recent events seemed such a setback.

The present was right there, after all, pushing in on them enough to put Ruth in the hospital.

Skinny looked over at Ruth, but just for a moment, not really wanting to see.

When they had met, Ruth had been working in a real estate developer's office. Skinny had been working a case. He had needed to see the developer, so he had gone inside and announced, "This is Skinny," jabbing his forefinger against his own chest; but before he had been able to say what it was he wanted, Ruth had shot back, "This is Ruth," mimicking his gesture, pointing at herself with one long, red-nailed finger. "What can Ruth do for Skinny?" Skinny had rolled his eyes in reply, but he had known right away he would like her.

What can Ruth do for Skinny? Skinny repeated to himself, shaking his head, knowing what she had already done.

More than anything else, Ruth had given his life focus, a sense of purpose beyond putting one guy after another in jail. She had made him see the fun in things he would never before have considered—like going downriver to sort through the flotsam that had washed up on the batture. She had made him aware of small possibilities in even very simple things, things as simple as staying home for dinner or helping her clear out her patio. He felt somehow more complete just knowing she was there, a feeling that, in light of the day's events, he had to wonder whether or not she shared.

Skinny got up and moved the trash can near the armchair, placing it to use as a footrest.

When it had come right down to it, when Dwayne had asked her to meet him alone, she hadn't trusted him. That much was self-evident, and as he thought about it, trying to put it in context, he could see that lack of trust in other things as well. He could see it in the way she sat and looked out the window sometimes, her thoughts far away, remote and untouchable. He could feel it in the way she did some things, without asking for help even when help would make her task easier, constantly proving her self-sufficiency. He knew she had trouble with that—she had told him—but he had never before put it together with a basic lack of trust. He'd never had reason to.

He tried to cross his ankles on the rim of the trash can, but his boot slipped on the white plastic liner. The trash can nearly overturned.

What it came down to, he saw, was whether or not he could carry on in the face of a lopsided affection. Was he stronger than she was, able to trust without being wholly trusted himself? Did he want to?

Skinny shrugged, a slight motion of his shoulders that caused him to slide down in the chair.

Skinny's just Skinny, he said to himself. *The rest of it is Ruth's problem.* He slid back up to a sitting position. *Skinny's Ruth's problem, too*, he added, a thought that perked him up right away. *He sure isn't leaving.*

Ruth tossed about in her sleep, changing position.

Skinny reached through the bars on the guardrail and put his hand on her forearm, staying right where he was.

Several hours later, Skinny heard, "*Pssst, Pssst*," and looked around to see Agent Gatzke, just his head stuck through the door, one hand beneath it waving him out into the hall.

Immediately aggravated, Skinny jumped up and threw the door open wide.

"What?" he said loudly enough that the nurse at the station stared at him over her clipboard.

"*Shhh,*" Gatzke said, one finger to his lips, placating the nurse. He motioned for Skinny to follow him to the visitors' lounge at the end of the hall.

Skinny followed, but as soon as they were in the lounge, he said, "What?" again, just as loudly.

Gatzke smiled, revealing his small teeth.

"You got my supplemental report written yet?" he asked, obviously joking, obviously trying to break the ice. "Just kidding," he added, then he pointed over his shoulder with his thumb. "You want some coffee?"

Skinny shook his head no, and Gatzke turned to the coffee-vending machine, put in two quarters, punched two buttons.

"I'm sorry about Ruth," he said as a paper cup dropped into place then filled with a curiously colored yellow-brown liquid. "How is she?"

"She'll be okay," Skinny replied. He dug into his pocket for change, went past Gatzke, and got himself two cream-filled chocolate cakes in a pack. He unwrapped the cakes and took a big bite, waiting to see what Gatzke had on his mind; but Gatzke seemed content just to stand there, holding the cup of coffee to his lips and blowing across the top of it.

"The pistol you mentioned?" he said finally. "The one you saw on the boat? I have seen one like it."

"Yeah?" Skinny remarked, and took another big bite of cake. The cream squished out and smeared his upper lip. "So?" he added, and wiped his mouth with the back of his hand.

"The guns were stolen from an army storage facility in Maryland," Gatzke went on. "We recovered some of them. The rest are still missing." He made a face at the taste of the coffee. "The people who sell this"—he looked with distaste into the cup—"ought to be arrested."

"Even Skinny won't drink it," Skinny acknowledged.

"Evans Charles was running guns on his boat," Gatzke said, and put the cup of coffee into the trash.

"Taking guns out and bringing drugs back, right?" Skinny asked, quickly putting it together. "That way there's no wasted gas."

"Maybe," Gatzke conceded, searching in his pocket for more change. "That's what the DEA claims anyway." He held the contents of his pocket on his palm and looked through them. "I think the DEA is full of shit." He picked out two coins and rattled them together. "I think they just want a piece of my case." His eyes flicked from one vending machine to the next. "I do the work. They claim at least part of the credit."

"That's not what they say," Skinny replied easily. He looked at the clear plastic wrapper his cakes had come in, saw the icing that had stuck to it, and began to lick it off. "They say you haven't got a case anymore," he said between licks. "Evans Charles is dead. You're out on your butt."

Gatzke put his quarters into the machine out of which Skinny had gotten his cakes, but when he pushed a button, nothing happened.

"I went to see 'em," Skinny explained. He wiped his mouth with his hand then wiped that hand on his jeans. "It was their man who beat up Ruth—I'm going to see that asshole, too."

"They told you that?" Gatzke asked, vigorously working the coin-return lever. "They told you it was their man?"

Skinny shook his head side to side.

"Ruth saw him." He wadded up the plastic wrapper and put it into an ashtray nearby. "Ruth and I both saw him last night. He was one of the guys who followed us when we left the Silver Lily."

"No shit," Gatzke said when both his coins were returned. He put the coins in his pocket, apparently deciding not to risk them again. "Their problem is, they've never been able to find any drugs."

"Ishanti is good for drugs," Skinny noted.

"I didn't say that he wasn't good for them," Gatzke replied. "I said they haven't been able to find them." Gatzke leaned back against the vending machine into which he had put his quarters. "And it's not like they should have to look that hard." He leaned back farther, using the weight in his beefy shoulders, forcing the machine onto two legs.

"Do you know Ishanti?" Skinny asked.

"No," Gatzke admitted. "I've never had the pleasure." He stepped forward, allowing the machine to come forward with him, then pushed it back again, rocking it until it bumped the wall.

"He'd never touch drugs himself," Skinny said. "He'd use someone else."

When Gatzke allowed the heavy machine to come forward again, it rocked too far forward and started to fall over on its face.

"Son of a bitch," he said as, in taking the weight, trying to prop the machine up and keep it from falling, he realized just how heavy it was.

"You won't get anything," Skinny predicted, before he moved in to help.

Gatzke cut his eyes at him in a pained look.

"Skinny's tried rocking machines before."

With some effort, together they were able to push the machine back onto its feet. Not a single item had fallen from the display rack into the chute.

"You might have said something," Gatzke complained.

"I could have been wrong," Skinny replied. "I've been wrong before. Try your quarters again," he suggested.

Gatzke put his hands in his pockets but did not come out with his change.

"The boy is at risk," he said, his tone somber. "We've got to find the boy."

"Dwayne," Skinny corrected him, a little annoyed, finally realizing why Gatzke was there: he was trying to find out what Skinny had learned because he hadn't learned anything himself. Not that, as Skinny then put it together, he should be really surprised. Gatzke had, after all, come to him twice before to get him to do his job, once when he had been out with his beeper somewhere and once when he had been with his ex-wife in Baton Rouge. He even wanted Skinny to write his report and needed Skinny's help to rock a vending machine. The guy was worse than Theriot—Theriot did, after all, at least try to do his own work.

"Dwayne," Gatzke conceded. "We've got to find Dwayne."

"I'm here to visit Ruth," Skinny said, making it obvious he was getting ready to leave.

"You'll call me, huh?" Gatzke said.

"I'll call you," Skinny agreed, though as he went back down to the hall to Ruth's room, he was happy to note that he hadn't said when.

19

Skinny dozed in the armchair beside Ruth's bed, then when he was sure it was late enough, he got up and left. He went to Ruth's car and took it across the river, going exactly the same way he had before when he and Ruth had taken Dwayne to Agnes.

The parking area in front of the Silver Lily Club was empty. The Monday-night crowd, as Skinny had hoped, by midnight had already gone home to bed. Inside he saw the rosy pink lights were still on, so he got out and went in, going a little slower this time, looking in as he pulled open the door, checking it out. Empty, the Silver Lily Club was very different, just another bar that smelled of stale cigarette smoke, beer, and pine-scented disinfectant. In the back, he heard the rough, scraping sound of ice being scooped.

Skinny glanced out the dark, mirrored door before he went forward and stood at the bar, one foot up on the rung of a stool, his forearms on the bar itself. A minute or two later, the bartender appeared through a curtained doorway carrying a filled plastic trash can, holding it against his massive gut. He eyed Skinny coldly, then studiously ignored him as he began to pour ice into the coolers behind the bar.

"Where is everybody?" Skinny asked. "I'm not sure whether I should stay for a drink."

The bartender went on as he had before, simply pretending that Skinny wasn't there, pouring ice into the coolers one at a time; but Skinny saw his eyes glancing up furtively. When the trash can was empty, he turned away, moving deliberately. When he turned back, he was holding a meat cleaver, a big one, with a thick, tarnished blade and a heavy wooden handle. With his free hand, he took an orange from one of the coolers.

"I know you," the man said, and with a pounding motion cut the end off the orange. The cleaver thumped against the bar. A round piece of peel stuck to the blade. "Saw you in here before, know you police." The cleaver thumped again. "Ain't got much use for police."

"I know you, too," Skinny replied cheerfully. Timing his move carefully, he reached over and grabbed the slice of orange the man had chopped off. He folded the slice and bit into the pulp, chewing contentedly. "Good orange," he observed. "Sweet."

The bartender looked at him questioningly, his dark eyes squinting malevolently.

"How you know me?" he asked.

Using both hands, Skinny pushed the slice of orange against his front teeth to gnaw in close to the rind.

"I'm no doctor," Skinny replied, "but I know an asshole when I see one."

The bartender glared at him, the meat cleaver held above the bar, poised, poised but uncertain.

Skinny reached over and took a cherry from the open

compartmentalized condiment tray on the bartender's side of the bar.

"Skinny likes knives," he went on. "Knives and meat cleavers. He likes people to carry them." He swallowed the first cherry and helped himself to another. "All he's got to do is to backpedal fast enough to get to his gun." He smiled brightly. "But I'd rather just talk."

The bartender lifted the meat cleaver and chopped it straight down, cleanly slicing the orange but, as Skinny saw it, coming dangerously close to his fat, round fingers.

"What's your name anyway?" he asked.

"Henry," the man replied sullenly as he continued to chop. Using the slablike side of the blade, he moved the first orange out of the way and reached for another.

Skinny unzipped his jacket enough that he could get to his gun.

"So, Henry," Skinny went on casually, taking another slice of orange, "why'd you drop a dime on Agnes and the boy?"

Henry stopped what he was doing and looked up. His black eyes were very small in his face, small and veiled, but alert.

"Didn't drop no dime on nobody," he said.

"It had to be you," Skinny argued easily. "You're the only one who knew I was bringing the boy back. I called, remember? Whoever you told was waiting for them."

Henry held the meat cleaver flat against the bar.

"Me and Agnes, we got along good. Wouldn't do her no harm—want to find out who killed her myself."

"You're the only one who knew," Skinny repeated. "You and whoever you told."

Henry began his chopping again, put off and apparently thinking, so Skinny changed direction.

"What about Evans Charles? You know him?"

"He come in sometimes," Henry replied. "Come in off the river. Drink beer. Don't leave no tip."

"How do you know he came in off the river?"

"The river got a smell. Smell it on him."

Henry finished with oranges and took out two lemons and a lime. Skinny watched as he began to chop them, chopping the cleaver within fractions of an inch of his fingers. For a while Skinny was mesmerized by the sure, quick motion of the big blade. He felt each thump vibrating in the bar, and only after the first lemon had been cleanly cut into slices did he realize that what Henry was doing was not some sort of act but something he did every night, proprietarily preparing for opening the next day.

"So who owned this place before Ishanti?" he asked, drawing the obvious conclusion. "You?"

"It my place," Henry affirmed. "I started it." He glanced up long enough to catch Skinny's eye. "Me and Agnes."

"I'm sorry, Henry," Skinny said, meaning it, picking up on the hurt in Henry's expression. "I'm sorry about Agnes."

Henry kept chopping, but his pace seemed to change just a bit. The tension went out of his wrist and he let the weight of the blade do the work. For the first time Skinny watched him rather than the cleaver, noting his big chest and shoulders and bigger Buddha-like stomach beneath, his gray work pants and white T-shirt and the bar rag tucked in at his waist. He could picture Henry and Agnes together. He could almost hear the gruff, good-natured exchanges between them. He could sense their easy familiarity, Agnes coming in to work every day and Henry every once in a while going out to the shack on the river. He knew the emptiness inside him.

When Henry finished chopping, he put the cleaver away. He took out a small knife and methodically began to cut the slices into quarters.

"They beat the shit out of Ruth," Skinny said. "Ruth is Skinny's Agnes."

Henry glanced up, then down at the knife in his hand. He continued to quarter the slices, the knife flashing between his fingers, and as each slice was completed, he used the side of the blade to push the drink-sized wedges out of the way. After a while, he said, "Ishanti come in here one day, say he want the Silver Lily, say he want to buy it. He offer me five thousand dollars." One piece of lemon did not cut all the way through, and he cut it again. "He say I can still work here, but he got some changes he need to make. He say he need the place for his business." The knife blade scraped on the bar. "I say, the Silver Lily the only thing I got. It mine. Don't want no kind of trouble. He say, take the money, Henry. He say he like me. Don't want to have to burn the place down."

Henry gathered up the wedges separately and put them with the other wedges in the condiment tray on the bar.

"What I tell Agnes, a man like Ishanti, he not going to be around for long. Got too many like him. We hold on, we have the money after he gone—have the Silver Lily, too. I say maybe I get her a color TV. She ain't never had one. Maybe get her a new coat."

Skinny knew what Agnes's response had been, because in her small house there was no TV.

Henry rinsed the knife in a sink filled with soapy water then put it away. In the bar, Skinny noted the deep, bowl-like hollow his nightly chopping and slicing had made.

"What kind of business?" Skinny asked, though he felt he already knew. "Drugs?"

Henry did not reply right away but began to wipe down the bar with a rag.

"Never seen no drugs," he replied finally. "Just seen the people."

"Like the guy I saw back there?" Skinny asked, jerking his head to one side, indicating the booth at the back of the room. "The guy who had the bird on his shoulder?"

Henry nodded slightly as he continued to wipe down the bar, working his way from one end to the other.

"His name Nickel," Henry said. "He in here when I open, doing his business. Ishanti's business. He in here when you called, heard me talking to you, heard you bringing back the boy." He looked over almost furtively, glancing at Skinny out of the corner of one eye. "He in here last night, too. You seen him. He follow you when you leave, want to see what you up to."

Skinny thought about that for a moment, feeling a cool hardness run up his spine. When Henry got near, he took his arms off the bar.

"Nickel? Is that what he's called?" he asked, wanting to be sure he had the name right, because Henry had just told him who had beaten up Ruth.

"Nickel," Henry affirmed, "like you got in your pocket."

Skinny had never really seen who it was who had followed Ruth and him. He had seen the car, all right, but he had not looked out the window like Ruth had, blatantly checking them out. He had been content with his quick glimpses in the rearview mirror, confident that he would have the car stopped soon enough.

"What's his real name?" he asked.

"Anthony," Henry replied. "Don't know his last name." He finished wiping down the bar and moved out from behind it. He went to the booths along the wall and began to wipe them down, too.

Skinny stayed where he was, one foot up on the rung of a stool, one hand grasping its back. He could feel his brain ticking, slotting things into place, and he let his thoughts go, feeling as though he was learning things himself. Maybe Nickel had blown up the boat. Maybe not. But likely enough he knew about the explosion— and its intent—and after he learned that Dwayne was alive and Skinny was bringing him back, he only had to walk about two hundred yards to wait near Agnes's shack. And after that, after missing the boy and killing Agnes, all he had to do was to double back to the Silver Lily to have an unimpeachable account of where he had been—and to see Skinny again. Skinny worried him. So he had followed Skinny's truck long enough to be certain he was really leaving the area, then the next day he had caught up to Ruth. He had beaten her because it accomplished two things at once: she *might* have told him about Dwayne, and the beating left a message for Skinny.

"That makes sense," Skinny said out loud, a remark that caused Henry to glance in his direction as he wiped his way to the last booth.

"You ever see another white guy in here?" Skinny asked, asking about William Dryden, thinking of what he had said and his certainty that his man had killed no one. "Blond hair? Wears glasses? Probably had on a tie?"

"You the only white man I seen in here *ever*," Henry replied, his tone adding, "Most white men must have better sense"—a message that was lost completely on Skinny. He leaned down to pick something up, and when he stood up, Skinny saw it was a feather.

"I like that bird," Skinny remarked. "Where did he get it?"

"You not like it so much," Henry replied. "you got to clean up behind it."

Henry finished wiping down the last booth, went behind the bar, and threw his rag in the trash. He looked around critically, then began to turn off the lights.

"Last call, right?" Skinny remarked.

"Ain't got no last call," Henry replied. "Just close up when everyone go home."

Skinny made no objection to that and moved as Henry did toward the front door.

"Where do you live?" Skinny asked, going on outside. "You need a ride?"

Henry pulled shut the door and took out his keys.

"Usually stay here," he said. "Got a place upstairs." He locked the door and tested it by shaking the handle. "Goin' to Agnes's tonight. Got to go through her things."

Henry gave Skinny a brief glance that was questioning and self-conscious—and somehow reluctant. Then he walked away, cutting across the parking lot at an angle.

Skinny got into Ruth's car, started the engine, and watched Henry as he walked toward the levee. His short legs seemed to rock him side to side as much as to carry him forward. His broad shoulders seemed to sag, as if he were carrying great weight. At the base of the levee he paused for a moment, then he went on up it, leaning into the effort, his hands pushing down on his knees, not so much going forward as putting steps behind him.

"Jesus Christ," Skinny said softly, under his breath, looking away. He tucked his lower lip between his teeth and bit down on it, his bright, shrewd eyes looking past the Silver Lily, coming back to the business at hand. He felt fairly certain he could catch up to Nickel whenever he wanted—he just had to wait at the bar—but who he really wanted to see was Ishanti, to go right to the source; and while he did not know where to find him, he did know just who could tell him.

20

In Agnes's shack it was damp, damp and chilly and dark. Various smells intermixed, the smell of creosote and the smell of the river and the smell of the exposed felt paper that sealed up the roof and the walls. Faintly, behind those pungent chemical smells, there was Agnes's smell, almost a presence, musty and overlaid with face powder. Every once in a while, when a freighter or tanker or barge went by, waves lapped against the pilings that supported the shack. Irregularly, a river rat scurried on the joists beneath the rough floor. The plastic that covered one window rustled in the light breeze.

In the rear room of the shack, Dwayne sat in his auntee's large, overstuffed chair, his knees drawn up to his chest, his father's revolver within easy reach on the cushion beside his feet. He had been sitting like that for over two hours, tired but afraid to sleep, trying to figure out what had happened but his thoughts digressing, coming in waves of feeling of fear and helplessness and anger that intermixed like the smells in the room, each one distinct yet indistinguishable, too, running together. He did not know what to do. He did not know where it was safe or who he could trust. Regularly, he picked up the revolver and aimed it. He liked its good solid weight, its heft in his hand. He did not feel so helpless then or so much afraid. He was cold, and he shivered, drawing his knees in even more tightly to his chest.

In his mind, Dwayne saw the fourth floor apartment where he had lived with his mother and father. From the fire escape, he saw the unrelieved plainness of the brick walls dropping down, the people sitting on stoops and leaning on the sills to look out their own windows, the worn-down-to-earth courtyard below. Voices carried up to him in greetings and arguments and laughter. At three years old, he was a watcher. He could see inside his mind then. He could feel his powerlessness and his fear.

There were two men, one on either side of his mother, making her go. He could not see them clearly, but they were dark, big as giants, too strong. He hid behind the bathroom door, and through the crack between the door and the doorjamb he saw when they passed. He saw how they had handcuffed her hands behind her. She was yelling at them, raging. In his older mind he was able to rearrange what had actually happened and he stepped out from behind the door, into the hallway, and unhesitatingly he shot the first man in the back, down low so that he arched, his arms and his belly thrown out. The second man turned, and he shot him, too, in the chest and the throat, savoring the man's look of surprise. He shot and he shot until the gun would not shoot anymore. He liked that, the way it made him feel, adult, in control; and he replayed that scene a dozen times at least, changing it each time because he could never get it just right—because after that, while he knew his mother had not left, not then, not after what he had done to save her, still she wasn't there anymore. She was gone, disappeared somehow, gone but not like before. He ran to the door. He stopped. He saw his mother on the ground forty feet below. He had enough sense to run, to run to his father, a child once more—later, he would come back to her again.

For a while he had lived with his auntee, then when his father got the boat, he lived there, too, on the water. His father had been decent to him, showing him how the boat worked and letting him help with the painting and the repairs, but he knew, more often than not, he was just in the way, an unwelcome guest. And he knew, as a child knows, that there was something wrong about the boat, something that needed to be hidden, so very early on he had learned to lie about it, to keep the secret. He had learned to lie about other things, too— he had learned to stay up in his head where things could be arranged as he pleased, where he had control. Sometimes, he wanted to be mute so he would not have to speak. He did not like words, the way people questioned you with them, how they made you think. It was better not to have to explain things, the outbursts of temper he did not always understand himself or the way he got lost sometimes up in his head. Now his father and his auntee, they were both gone, and he didn't as yet understand what had happened, how he had let them slip away, too. It had to be him, his fault. It had to. He was the only one left. He knew with certainty what death was. He knew what that meant. He knew the strength that was his when he was able to separate his thoughts and emotions.

Don't matter, he said to himself, liking the way *those* words made him feel, the steely, cold hardness inside him—cold and hard as the gun in his hand, indistinguish-able from it, indistinguishable from *him*, one and the same. In his mind he was ready to use it again, on his auntee's killer this time, on his father's; but before he could, outside he heard slow and steady steps on the walkway.

For a moment he froze, not afraid but confused, then quickly he jumped out of the chair, taking the revolver with him, crouching down near the back door, listening, listening and ready.

The footsteps stopped near the front of the shack. A man's voice muttered. The generator was cranked, the rope pulled, then was cranked again and caught, the motor beginning its familiar hammering drone.

Dwayne ducked back behind the chair as the lights came on, knowing he would not be able to hear the foot-steps over the sound of the motor.

The front door opened and closed.

The man seemed to pause in the front room before he came back, his heavy movements halting and uncertain. After a while, Dwayne risked a look out and saw Henry standing in front of his auntee's big chest of drawers, a framed photograph held in both hands. He watched as Henry just looked at the picture, his expression blank and unformed. Finally, he put the photograph back on top of the dresser. He seemed about to open one of the drawers, but instead he came over and tiredly sat in the chair Dwayne had just left, the chair behind which Dwayne was still hiding.

In the dim light Dwayne could see the side of his big, beefy arm. He could hear his raspy, forced breathing, and when he felt ready he just stepped out in front of him—savoring his look of surprise.

It took Henry a moment to register the fact that Dwayne was right there.

"What you doin' here, boy?" Henry asked. "They lookin' all over for you."

Dwayne knew better than to answer any questions.

"Who lookin'?" he demanded to know.

"The policemen, for one," Henry replied.

"Ain't done nothin' wrong," Dwayne said.

"Ain't nobody said you done nothin' wrong. Just want to be sure you okay."

Dwayne knew that wasn't the whole answer. He could sense it.

"Who else lookin'?" he wanted to know. "Who killed my father?"

Rather than reply right away, Henry sat forward in the chair.

Dwayne took a cautious step back.

"I'm Henry," Henry said. "Known you since you were little. You ain't got no reason to be scared of me."

When Dwayne did not seem reassured by his words, Henry looked down, between his fat knees, pausing before he said anything else; and when at the edge of his vision he saw Dwayne move, he looked up, into the barrel of the revolver pointed right at his face.

"Who else lookin'?" Dwayne asked him again. "Who killed my father?"

During the time he had been at the Silver Lily Club, Henry had scuffled with more than his share of mean drunks. Twice he had stood off armed robbers. He had been stabbed and beaten and had even seen a man killed in front of him, but looking at those eyes behind the revolver, he had never felt so close to death. Dwayne's dark eyes were at the same time alert and very flat, removed, off somewhere else, utterly without any trace of human emotion. He knew, just by looking, he would kill him.

What been done to you, boy? he asked himself, before he tried as best he could to answer the questions.

21

Not far from the Silver Lily, near where the two-lane street that ran in front of it intersected the West Bank Expressway, there was a waffle house that stayed open all night. Skinny saw the restaurant's bright yellow sign and brightly lit parking lot and turned in. He parked well away from the few other cars in the lot, used the pay phone near the door to call the police, then went inside and got two cups of coffee to take out. He carried the coffee to Ruth's car, set the white, Styrofoam cups down on the hood, leaned back against the low fender. After a while, he opened one coffee and sipped it, looking around as he always did when he was out on the street, not wanting anyone to approach unless he saw them well in advance. A few minutes later, he saw the marked police car turn into the lot in response to his call, and he waved, summoning the officer over.

The police car approached slowly, then stopped, not turning into a parking space but staying in the middle of the lot.

"This is Skinny," Skinny said as the officer got out of

the car. He made a show of patting his pockets, searching for his ID.

"I saw you last night," the officer replied, "at the scene."

The policeman was shorter than average but well built, compact. His hair was dark red and curly, and although his features showed he was black, his skin was light with dark brown freckles. He wore tinted glasses with gold frames. Skinny handed him the second cup of coffee, and as he did so glanced at the name tag on the man's shirt.

"You're Freeman, right?"

Freeman had seen Skinny's glance and did not say anything. He looked at his coffee as he sipped it, just waiting; so Skinny went right to the point.

"I need to find a guy named Ishanti." When that name did not seem to register, he added, "He used to be called Big Jerome."

"I know who Ishanti is," Freeman replied.

"I figured you would," Skinny noted. "You work a beat, you meet all the headliners, right?"

In the bright light from the halogen lamps Skinny noticed that Freeman's uniform was exceptionally neat and well pressed. His black shoes and black belt were highly shined. The fact that he wasn't saying much put him off just a bit, but he had the sense that by his no-nonsense demeanor and his impeccable appearance Freeman was, out of habit, making a point.

"You live here, don't you?" Skinny asked, taking a guess. "You live in the same beat you work."

Freeman's eyes jumped to his, and Skinny knew that he had hit home.

"I did the same thing," Skinny remarked, "before I went to the bureau."

"Someone," Freeman noted, "has to show that there's another way to live beside Ishanti's."

Skinny admired him for that but decided not to say so.

"Have you found Dwayne?" Freeman asked.

Skinny shook his head no.

"We're looking. We will. We're hoping he'll come to us."

"He won't," Freeman predicted. "He won't come to you—you'll have to find *him*." He adjusted his belt by lifting up on his revolver, his eyes blank but casting about, as if looking for some point to latch onto.

"You know him?" Skinny asked.

"I know him," Freeman replied. "I was there when his mother died." He looked right at Skinny. "So was he."

Skinny crossed his arms on his chest then rubbed his chin, waiting for the story.

Freeman took a final sip of his coffee then placed the cup beside him on the hood of the car.

"The call came out to meet a narcotics officer in the parking lot of the Villa d'Ames." Freeman pointed in a way that indicated the housing project in the darkness down the street. "It was midafternoon. January. Overcast but not cold. I rode with a partner then. He was senior—I'd been out on the street less than a year."

"How long ago?" Skinny asked.

"Seven years," Freeman replied, his mouth a tight, serious line. "So we met up with the guy from narcotics. He had a bullshit warrant on a guy who had missed a court date—he was plainclothes, and all he wanted was a couple of uniforms with him so there would be no mistake about who he was. Nothing to it. We knock on the door, and if the guy's not there, that's that. If he is there, we arrest him." He shrugged. "We go up to the fourth floor, find the apartment, and knock on the door. We wait, no answer. We're about to leave when the door finally opens. There's a woman standing there with a syringe in her arm. She's tied off and shooting up while she answers the door."

"Jesus," Skinny remarked.

"No one moved. The three of us just stood there, not even believing it. How stupid can you be, right? The woman doesn't look away from her arm. She starts to go on the nod right there, the needle still in the crook of her arm. The narcotics guy finally says something, she looks up—and she goes mental. Dwayne's mother. He was in the next room."

"Terrific," Skinny remarked, wondering what perverse impulse had prompted the woman to open the door—but he had met enough junkies to know that there wasn't an answer.

"It took all three of us to pin her down long enough to put on the cuffs. The woman is screaming and kicking the whole time. We're holding her face down on the couch. The neighbors hear the noise and come out on the walkway. It's a mess."

Freeman's words trailed off then took on a renewed, harder strength.

"We know we have to get her out of there, into the car, or we're going to have a riot. The guy from narcotics goes out first to try to get the neighbors out of the way. My partner and I lift her off the couch and go out behind him. We each have an arm. She's between us. We make it as far as the stairs."

Using his thumb and first finger, Freeman adjusted his glasses.

"She fights us every inch of the way. She's kicking, bucking, twisting around, cursing the whole time. I'm not really sure whether she threw herself at the handrail or just slipped. But the result was the same: she went over."

"Off the walkway?"

Freeman nodded.

"Forty feet onto concrete."

"Shit," Skinny said, the image of what had happened very clear in his mind. He had had calls like that himself, calls that should have been simple that very quickly got out of hand. He saw the woman on the concrete, forty feet below, her hands still handcuffed behind her, and he understood two things at once. He understood why, seven years later, Freeman was still in uniform working a beat, and he understood why Dwayne had told Ruth not to bring the police.

"I keep up with Dwayne," Freeman went on. "I see him, I stop to say hello. I used to go by where he lived, but his aunt asked me to stop. She said it upset him."

"It's the uniform," Skinny offered. "Everybody remembers the uniform."

Freeman shook his head, as if he didn't think so.

"Last year, I got called over to the middle school. It's about five blocks from here. His aunt sends him. Sometimes he goes, sometimes he doesn't." Freeman shrugged. "The day I went, Dwayne had beaten up one of his classmates so badly I had to take the little boy to the hospital." Freeman's eyes were steady on Skinny's. "He won't come to you."

Skinny accepted that, thinking it over, putting it together with what he already knew—and fitting it to Freeman, the too-ready way he had related the story.

"Don't beat yourself to death with it," he advised. "It wasn't your fault."

"It was the wrong apartment," Freeman replied. "The apartment number on the warrant was wrong—we never should have knocked on that door in the first place."

"Shit," Skinny said again because he didn't know what else he *could* say.

"Shit," Freeman repeated.

Skinny ran his hand through his hair, front to back, and looked past Freeman, his quick glance taking in the whole parking lot. Two men came out of the waffle house and got into a truck. The truck backed out and then, in deference to the marked police car blocking the way, exited the lot through the entrance.

"What about Ishanti?" Skinny asked. "I need to find him."

Freeman looked right at him, his gaze curious and hard, as if questioning Skinny's comprehension of the story he had just told. After a moment, he looked away and changed position, leaning back and putting one foot up on the bumper of the police car.

"Ishanti is hard to predict. I don't see him for a week, then I see him three or four days in a row."

"At the Silver Lily?"

Freeman nodded.

"There, or just around."

"He has to sleep somewhere."

"He has to sleep somewhere," Freeman agreed.

There was something about Freeman that made Skinny nervous, some quality to the unblinking directness of his gaze. Freeman, he decided, was swimming pretty close to the deep end. Skinny patted his pockets, found his wallet, took out a card that he stepped up and handed to Freeman.

"Call me the next time you see Ishanti. Let me know where he's at."

Freeman glanced at the card briefly, then put it away in his shirt pocket.

"I shot someone once by mistake," Skinny lied. "There are people you can see to help you get past it."

"I've never shot anyone," Freeman replied.

Skinny shrugged, raising and dropping both his shoulders at once, knowing full well that, when you don't want to help yourself, there's no one around who can help you.

"I'll be in touch," he said, and turned to get into Ruth's car. He started the engine, put the car in gear, drove out of the lot, noticing in the rearview mirror that Freeman was just where he had been, unmoving, apparently looking at some point in the middle distance.

22

Despite his temptation to go by the hospital again, from the waffle house Skinny went home—he knew that, whether or not Ruth was actually asleep, as late as it was she *should* be, and a visit from him would not allow her the rest she needed. He parked Ruth's car beside his truck, went up to his apartment, and without even thinking about it turned on the TV. He took off his boots and stretched out on the couch, took out his silver gun and unloaded it, and began to click away, idly shifting his aim from his big toe to the black-and-white images on the late-night movie.

Freeman's story about Dwayne's mother spooked him. So much, it seemed, happened as a result of pure chance: a secretary had typed a wrong number, Freeman had knocked on the wrong door as a result, and whole lives had changed forever—which wasn't all that much different from what had happened to Ruth and him. They had been out looking for driftwood, a boat had exploded nearby . . . and what? Their lives were changed, that much was for certain, but how?

A commercial came on, interrupting the movie, and Skinny aimed and fired at a big box of breakfast cereal.

In the relations he had before had with women, Skinny had learned the importance of a parallel sort of growth. With a woman, he had learned, you had to share and assimilate life's experiences together, in a reasonably similar sort of way, because if you didn't there could be a change of direction by one or the other and the very real danger of growing *apart*.

The breakfast cereal was replaced by a bottle of beer, and he shot at that, too.

Ruth and he had shared an experience that, though in fact pretty much the same for them both, was affecting them differently. Ruth was seeing a part of life she had never before seen, that same part he happened to understand very well. And the big question was, was she catching up, coming up on a parallel track—did she understand what he did—or was she growing away?

Skinny put the bullets back into his gun, turned off the TV, went upstairs, and went to bed. What he knew for a fact was, for him the hardest thing of all was simply to hold on, to wait for the other shoe to drop.

23

Ishanti was just past the intersection of Ames Boulevard and the West Bank Expressway, past the McDonald's and Brown's Lounge, heading away from the active, brightly lit area into the darker and quieter area of the housing project, when in his rearview mirror he saw headlights flash onto bright. It was just after three in the morning. For a fraction of a second, red police-bar lights flashed, too—a signal not an order—and he looked in the mirror more closely, not alarmed, just making sure, verifying the sihouette of the police car behind him. He eased onto the shoulder of the road and stopped but did not get out of his car, preferring instead to wait, to let the officer come up to him, to see who he was.

The police car stopped farther out into the street than he had stopped his car, and in the side-view mirror Ishanti saw the officer get out and start forward. He saw the shield-shaped decal on the open car door. When the officer came up past the police car's headlights, he recognized the man, and Ishanti got out, too, moving easily and deliberately, more curious than concerned.

Ishanti was dressed casually but expensively in pleated

tan pants and an Italian-cut short-sleeved gray shirt. The shirt's fabric was patterned with small white designs, fifties-style. A lizard-skin belt a foot too long looped back, tucked under itself, and although the fit of the clothes was very loose and casual, still it was impossible not to notice his very physical presence. Massive, thick legs supported a torso that was without real definition, not pretty or built-up but big, big and thick. His neck seemed to be without shape as well and went straight up, shoulders to ears. His ears were set in close to his head. Dark eyes under a broad, sloping brow moved quickly and easily, with the unself-conscious confidence of pure physical power.

Freeman, the policeman who had stopped him, stayed away from him, close enough to talk but a few feet out into the street.

"I see you around here," Freeman began, the rhythm of his speech more pronounced, different than when he had spoken with Skinny. "I know what you do."

Ishanti did not reply but waited for Freeman to go on, his black eyes steady and unwavering.

"Got no problem with you."

Ishanti acknowledged that with a barely perceptible movement of his head.

"A detective is looking for you. He told me to call him when I see you." Freeman stepped forward and handed Ishanti Skinny's card. "Now I've seen you, and I'm going to make the call."

Ishanti did not look at the card but kept his eyes on Freeman, recognizing right away the thin line he was walking. After a moment, Ishanti looked down on purpose, granting him the measure of respect that was due him.

"Tall, skinny white cop?" Ishanti asked, after he had glanced at the card. "Talks loud?"

Freeman nodded.

Ishanti tapped the card against the open palm of his hand.

"I know him," he acknowledged.

He started to wonder aloud why Skinny wanted to see him, but Freeman turned and walked off, back to the police car, and Ishanti let him go without asking the question. He put the card in his pocket and leaned back against the side of his car, idly watching as Freeman got into the police car and drove off.

Ishanti had been born in one of the apartments he could see in the housing project in front of him, and except for the time he had spent in jail, he had spent his whole life in and around there. He had gone to the local grammar school and junior high, then on to West Jefferson High School. Starting at fourteen, during the summers he had worked in the Avondale Shipyard—even then he had been big enough to pass for a man. His world held very few surprises, a situation he liked because the last time he had been truly surprised was when the judge had given him forty years straight up rather than probation. Freeman's stop—and the card now in his pocket—presented a dilemma he resolved a few minutes later. He got back into his car, drove to a pay phone nearby, and called the number. When he was told that Skinny wasn't there, he left a message that he would meet him at seven that evening. Thereafter, he went home and went to bed, only mildly concerned about what he could not control, unaware that, five hours later, the message he had left would give Skinny fits.

24

First thing the next morning, Skinny went back to the hospital. Ruth was already awake, sitting up in bed, her breakfast pushed off to one side. Skinny examined the remains of the food, selected a piece of bacon cooked to a questionably tan crisp, and sat at the foot of the bed to eat it.

"I missed breakfast," he explained.

Ruth smiled slightly because she knew what he was really saying.

"They'll let you out of here today," he predicted. "Tomorrow at the latest."

Ruth did not reply to that but looked away, out the window. When she looked back, Skinny was standing up again, reexamining her breakfast.

"Is there any word about Dwayne?" she asked, though she suspected that, if there were, he would already have told her.

"He'll show up soon," Skinny promised, because he felt certain he would. "The man who beat you?" he went on, purposely changing direction. "He's called Nickel. His real name is Anthony. Nickel works for a man called

Ishanti—Dwayne's father worked for Ishanti, too. Small world, right?"

Ruth's gaze remained on Skinny though, over the big bandage taped across her nose, her expression was vague, not so much uninterested as distanced. Skinny waited, idly chewing another piece of bacon, tasting its unusual saltiness, until the focus came back into her eyes.

"I didn't sleep very well last night," Ruth explained.

"It's the anesthesia," Skinny observed. "It gives you a hangover."

Ruth nodded agreement though it was obvious her thoughts were still somewhere else.

"Dwayne's not really the point," she said finally. "I mean, he is and he isn't—I *do* want you to find him. You *have* to." She paused, searching for words. "It's me, Skinny. I don't know what *I* want. Dwayne made me aware of my own confusion."

"About having kids?"

Ruth nodded.

"About that—and about other things. I always told my mother that if I ever got the urge to have children, I'd buy myself a cocker spaniel puppy." She smiled wanly, in a way that showed the uncertainty inside her, with no response to it possible, then her swollen-eyed gaze went back to Skinny. "Why do you call yourself Skinny? Why do you talk about yourself as if you were talking about someone else?"

Skinny was surprised by the question but not put off by it.

"Habit," he replied with a shrug. "I've been a policeman since I was twenty years old." He shrugged again, as if dismissing the last eleven years of his life, letting them go as just something he had done. "See, when you write a police report, you always use third person in the narrative. It avoids confusion. You write, 'We checked the building,' and somebody'll ask, '*Who* checked the building?' And it might be a year later before it gets to court and you have to remember. So you skip the pronouns. You write, 'The officer responded to the call and met with the owner. The officer and the owner made a search of the premises.' "

Ruth thought that over for a moment.

"So you write 'Skinny' instead of 'the officer'?"

"Only when I think I can get away with it." Skinny smiled. "Not too often." He put his hands in his pockets, then nudged the bed tray to one side with his elbow. "I always resented having to write about myself in the third person. It takes away your identity. It makes you sound like everyone else."

Ruth wanted to smile at that because, of all the things Skinny was, he certainly was *not* like anyone else, not like anyone she had ever met anyway; but he went on.

"There's another part of it, too, Ruth," he admitted. "Something we've never really gotten into."

Skinny hesitated, and Ruth knew instinctively what he was about to say—that part of her confusion she was not sure she *could* resolve.

"What I do when I go to work, it's different. Most of the time, it's not pretty. Or nice. You saw just a little piece of it, and it's thrown you. I saw how you looked when you saw Agnes Charles—you probably haven't even looked in the mirror yet and seen how *you* look." Before he went on, Skinny looked right at Ruth, with his glance trying to let her know that he wasn't pressing her for reassurance. "We all use different tricks on ourselves, ways to get through the day. A lot of times I say 'Skinny' because it puts me *out there*. It gives me some distance."

Ruth considered that, admitting to herself that she had

never really considered what Skinny did to cope, to get through his days.

"You know what Theriot does?" Skinny went on.

"Yes—" Ruth began, remembering what Mike Theriot had told her.

"That dumb bastard *daydreams*," Skinny overrode her. "Can you believe it? He gets this blank look and he's gone. Vacated. Out in space somewhere. It drives me nuts."

Ruth did smile then, thinly but genuinely.

The phone beside the bed rang quietly, a low tone more than a ring.

"What?" Skinny answered it. "We were just talking about you," Ruth heard him say. "It's Theriot," he explained, and looked at the clock on the table beside the bed. "I'm late for work." He listened intently for a moment, then said, "Run the rap sheet on that nervy bastard and bring it with you. Skinny'll meet you in ten minutes."

Ruth heard him revert to third person and the sound of it gave her pause. She heard the tension in his voice.

"You want to talk to Ruth?"

Apparently Mike Theriot did, because Skinny handed her the phone. She just held it and looked at him questioningly.

"That guy I was telling you about?" Skinny explained. "Ishanti?" In a gesture she recognized, he ran his hand through his hair, front to back. "That son of a bitch is out looking for *me*."

25

From the hospital Skinny made it to the detective bureau in eleven minutes flat, a time slightly less than it took Mike Theriot to make it down from the fourth floor by elevator. Skinny was waiting on the sidewalk, pacing three steps one way then three steps back the other, undecided about whether or not he had to go in, when he saw Theriot come out the door.

Theriot seemed a little reluctant to see him.

"The captain called me in," he explained. "He wanted to know where you were."

"What did you tell him?" Skinny asked, playing it cool.

In his right hand Mike Theriot was holding his fat plastic briefcase; in his left hand was his long chrome flashlight. That Tuesday morning he had on a baby-blue suit, white shirt, and wide one-color baby-blue tie.

"I told him you'd had a rough couple of days." He looked around for his car, spotted it, and headed that way. "He said okay that you were late if you were at the hospital; and he said to tell you not to get involved in a personal case." He put his briefcase on the hood of the car as he took out his keys. "How's Ruth?"

Skinny saw what Mike Theriot was doing—how he was minimizing the extra load he was carrying because his partner's attention was fixed somewhere else—and he appreciated it.

"Ruth is okay," he replied.

Mike Theriot unlocked the car, got in, reached over, and unlocked the passenger-side door for Skinny. He put his flashlight down beside his leg, lifted his briefcase onto the backseat, twisted around, and opened it.

"Ruth isn't so okay," Skinny admitted as he got in.

"That was my impression," Mike Theriot readily replied. He took out the folder he wanted and his clipboard and allowed himself to slide down, settling back onto the front seat. "She said to tell you not to worry, she'd work it out." He handed the folder to Skinny. "And she said to make sure you got some breakfast." He started the car and put it in gear. Before he drove off, he waited until Skinny glanced over. "She will work it out, Skinny."

"Yeah?" Skinny remarked, his tone expressing his uncertainty.

"Yeah," Mike Theriot countered, his tone expressing his confidence. "Think about it: *she's* in the hospital and still she's worried about *you* getting breakfast—you got no problems at all."

Skinny did think about it, and he liked how it felt.

"Thanks," he said.

Mike Theriot grinned in reply, obviously pleased by his own observation; and Skinny opened the folder on his lap, going right to Ishanti's rap sheet, surprised at how short it was. The computer readout showed only one arrest for armed robbery—and that had been thirteen years before.

"He's six six and two hundred fifty pounds," Mike Theriot noted when he saw what Skinny was reading.

"He's as big as a house," Skinny replied absently.

Clipped to the rap sheet was a pink message slip. "Outside the yard, seven P.M.," he read aloud.

Mike Theriot looked at him questioningly.

"The prison yard," Skinny explained, knowing intuitively what the message meant. In one way it made sense to meet at the prison—there were guards in the towers with high-powered rifles who would make sure they stayed reasonably friendly—but in another way, Skinny felt certain, Ishanti was giving him another sort of message, reminding him who had been in charge. "Ballsy bastard," he added.

"You know him?" Mike Theriot asked.

"I know him," Skinny affirmed.

Skinny glanced through his mail, found nothing of interest, started through his telephone messages. On top was a message from Freeman: "Saw Ishanti" was all that it said. "You bet," Skinny remarked. He looked up, looked around, saw that they *were* actually moving. "Where are we going for breakfast?"

In reply, Mike Theriot glanced at his watch then picked up his clipboard and handed it to Skinny.

Midcity, the preliminary report indicated, a man had been found, dead from an apparently self-inflicted gunshot wound to the head.

"How long has he been there?" Skinny asked.

Mike Theriot shrugged.

"The landlord found him—there were complaints about a smell."

Skinny made a sour face.

"That poor bastard won't mind if we stop on the way."

"He won't," Mike Theriot agreed, "but the landlord is waiting and she's plenty upset."

"Jesus Christ," Skinny remarked, momentarily wondering himself why he did what he did. "Before breakfast?"

"Maybe you ought to get up earlier," Mike Theriot offered.

Skinny did not dignify that with an answer but looked out the window, noting the rush-hour traffic, the bleary faces, reassuring himself that the situation could be far worse, before he went back to the messages in his hand.

His bank had called and so had his mother and a witness who had suddenly remembered a detail about a two-month-old murder. There was a reminder to pick up the boots he was having repaired and a request for him to make a contribution to the state troopers, to which he remarked, "Fat chance." The last message was from Henry, and before he read the message, without thinking he asked Mike Theriot who Henry was.

"The secretary must have gotten that one," Mike Theriot replied.

But when he looked back and read the message, Skinny knew immediately who Henry was, and he felt a chill run up his spine.

"The boy loose," Henry's message read. "He got a gun."

26

Between the plaster-covered brick footings, between the bottom of the house and the ground, in the open rectangular spaces someone a long time before had nailed up pieces of plywood to keep out stray dogs and cats and in the winter the wind. After Dwayne had left Henry sitting in Agnes's old chair, he had run down the levee and again hidden in the weeds on the batture; then a few hours later, just as first light had crept into the sky, enough to see, he had gone to the Silver Lily, flexed out a piece of that plywood, and crawled under the house. For the next few hours, he had worked himself into position, unhurriedly picking his way, low-crawling, putting aside half-buried bits of broken glass and old pieces of brick, removing dirt where he had to, watching his head. Near the center of the house, where there was very little clearance, a nail had snagged the small of his back; but he had not cried out.

Even with the sun now well up, it remained dark under the house. The light was a dim, eerie gray. Dwayne liked that. He liked the dark coolness. Wedged in, the floor joists solid against his back, he liked the feel of the dry, sandy dirt beneath him. He felt secure, and he slept, beginning his nap at just about the same time that Skinny was getting the message that he was loose and had a gun. He awoke when he heard footsteps over his head.

The day before, Dwayne had gone to the grocery and bought supplies for himself—a half dozen cans of Vienna sausage, potato chips, cookies, crackers, and a six-pack of soda—and he had carried them around in the tan plastic sack they had given him at the store. He took out a can of the sausage, opened it quietly, and began to eat. The fact that he had thought of food and provided it for himself made him feel good, adult, in a small way in control. He savored the last of the cookies before he moved forward enough to push out on the plywood to see where he was, pleased that he was only a few feet from where he wanted to be.

He took his time getting into position, getting it right. He moved forward the few feet he needed to, loosened the plywood, pushed it open, just a crack. Ten feet in front of him, to his left, was the single concrete step in front of the door to the Silver Lily. To his right was the parking lot, spread out between the front of the house and the street—down the street he could see the rise of the levee, the grass yellow-green in the late morning sun, and behind that in his mind's eye he could see his auntee's old shack.

Dwayne found a piece of brick with which he could hold open the plywood, put it in place to make sure it worked, then took it out. In the dim light, he scooped dirt into a small mound, patted it down, stretched out behind it. He scooped out a hollow for his chest and belly. Satisfied that he would be comfortable for the time he had to wait, he took out his father's revolver and sighted down the short barrel, using the mound as a rest.

"Coosh" was the soft sound he made, picturing Ishanti or Nickel, it didn't matter which. *"Coosh. Coosh."*

He opened the cylinder and checked the bullets, like he had seen them do on TV, then he put down the revolver and glanced around, looking for a route by which to escape.

27

The smell in the apartment was very nearly overwhelming, more than a smell, an olfactory force.

Before he did anything else, Skinny went to the kitchen, found a skillet and coffee, and purposely burnt the grounds until a thick, white smoke filled the apartment. The smell of the burnt coffee was acrid and raw—and enough to neutralize at least some of the smell of the decomposing body.

From the hallway outside the door, the landlady complained about the smoke detector's wail, so Skinny summarily removed the device from the ceiling.

Mike Theriot put on rubber gloves to go over the body, grateful that the man had had enough sense to use a small pistol on himself, rather than a rifle or shotgun.

The necessary reports made and the body finally removed, they went to get Skinny a late breakfast, though even Skinny's appetite was diminished somewhat by the smell that clung to their clothes. They spent the afternoon at the office, catching up on paperwork, including Gatzke's supplemental report, and in anticipation of the meeting with Ishanti that evening, Skinny went to his locker to retrieve his Louisville Slugger. Later on, he returned the bat to the locker because with one particularly fervent practice swing, misjudged just slightly, he launched a telephone on a collision course with a window and was saved from disaster only when the phone's cord pulled it up short. Mike Theriot was not as amused as he might have been otherwise since he had been using the phone at the time.

By early evening, Mike Theriot was hungry, so they went out to eat—Skinny left his bat in the car. And after hamburgers and coffee, just after dark, they went to the prison to get ready for the meeting with Ishanti.

28

The Orleans Parish Prison was overcrowded, holding far more men than its designers had ever intended, and one short-term solution, a federal judge had agreed, was to house the overflow prisoners in tents. So five years before, in what had been the exercise yard next to the prison, in the space of a week a tent city had been built. Dark green ten-man canvas tents were put up in rows, set as close together as their supporting ropes would allow. Between the rows were narrow wooden walkways, just wide enough for one man to pass. Around the small city was a high chain-link fence topped with a coil of shiny, silver, razor-sharp wire. In one corner was a guard tower that resembled a fire-watch tower.

Ishanti had heard about the tent city but had never actually seen it himself, a fact that, when he first saw it, made him realize he should have set the meeting for someplace else—this was not the yard he had known.

The street that ran beside the tent city was old and in disrepair, the potholes patched with shells. The streetlights gave off a burnt orange light that illuminated without making shadows. Ishanti made the block once before he parked near the corner. With the windows down, although the yard appeared abandoned, he could hear voices in the tents. In the tower he saw there were two men, their faces pale gray, lit by the light from video monitors. Sitting there looking out across the hood of his car brought him back to the time he had spent in the prison himself, when the area occupied by the tents had been an exercise yard—and to the time before that, to what had gotten him there.

What he remembered most from high school was the football stadium, its enormous stepped-concrete sides that held over fifteen thousand fans, and the spindly, powerful lights high above. He remembered stepping out onto the field in his brand-new blue-and-gold uniform, looking downfield at the opposing team, then at his own bench, seeing the coaches and the cheerleaders, hearing the roar from the crowd, knowing that he would dominate play as he had in every game before. Even at sixteen he was big and he was fast, and by the time he was eighteen and a senior he had filled out, putting on forty more solid pounds. No contest. He liked to hit and to hit hard, and when he was right he could knock flat a bulldozer. And even better than that, he had felt then, was after the games walking the halls in the school, walking slowly, one arm held rigid at his side, working his way forward around it, feeling cool, invincible, watching the crowd of students part in front of him, arriving at class whenever he chose because it just didn't matter—the rules didn't apply to him. He was Big Jerome. The star.

The star, Ishanti repeated to himself, in retrospect not at all surprised at what had come next.

Football was his ticket out, he had told his mother, the one person in his life who was not in awe of his status. Look what it had done for him already.

"Put foolishness in your head," she had replied. "Make you think you're more than you are."

So when the college recruiters had arrived, he had not allowed them to go to his mother's apartment or even to meet her but had met them in their motel rooms and at the school. They had promised him girls and cars and money, star status, and he had visited three colleges and almost immediately decided to go to the one where they had met him at the airport with a white limousine. He had signed the contract on the sun deck of a penthouse apartment, not even pretending to read it but watching the view and the girl the university had thoughtfully provided him, an accommodation that went along with the Jacuzzi and the fully equipped weight room. He was on top of the world and all he had to do was to wait, wait until late summer when practices began.

Ishanti saw movement near the corner of the yard and in the tower. In the dim light, he saw a rifle.

Wait, he said to himself, because in the years that had followed waiting was what he had learned to do best.

It had been hot the summer after graduation, hot and slow, the days in the project thick and heavy, monotonous; but the nights had been soft, much cooler, bearable though still monotonous and boring. Most evenings, when he had money, he bought a few quarts of beer and sat on the levee with his friends from the team, talking, getting rowdy, carrying on about how *bad* they had been. And if they didn't have money for more beer or ran out early, he would go down to the store and get more by asking for it, going right behind the counter and standing up real close to the clerk, letting him know who he was. He was Big Jerome. The star. He could do whatever he pleased— and what pleased him then was more Miller Lite. The store's owner tacitly agreed to the near-nightly proceedings, figuring a few quarts of beer were well worth maintaining peace in the neighborhood. Through June it went like that and into July, when the regular clerk was replaced temporarily by a Vietnamese who came equipped with his own .45.

At first, he hadn't noticed the new clerk but had gone to the cooler to get his three quarts of beer; on the way out, he had stopped by the counter and told the little man who he was. Language had been something of a problem, so he had just left, not explaining himself further, annoyed when the clerk had followed him outside. He had looked back only because the man was yelling, jabbering something he did not understand; and he was waving that big pistol, pointing it to emphasize whatever it was he was saying. Careful not to drop the three quarts of beer, he had grabbed the man's hand and the pistol and worked one loose from the other—and as far as he was concerned, that was that. Fifteen minutes later, the police had come up on the levee, the little clerk in tow, jabbering again, smiling meanly, and had found both the pistol and the three quarts of beer. The charge made against him was armed robbery, which had seemed like some kind of a joke until the policeman had told him he was looking at ninety-nine years.

Some joke.

The district attorney had a witness and a weapon and a forthcoming reelection, and had refused to reduce the charge. The judge had taken one look at him and had decided that, despite his lack of a previous record, he was capable of just about anything. And although he had kept in shape while he was in prison—using the exercise yard that now housed the tent city—when he got out football no longer appealed to him. He didn't pursue it—he didn't even watch the games on TV. He didn't want to think about that time in his life, because once he had reasoned it out, he had realized that, while he had dominated the play, the game, finally, had dominated him, a mistake he had sworn not to repeat. So now he tried to take the long view, to understand not just what he was doing that day but how each day's events fit into the long-term. He tried to plan as much as he could. He did not like surprises. He knew he would not go back to prison.

One of the two men in the tower stepped out onto the narrow walkway that ran around it. The man put one foot up on the railing and rested the butt of a rifle on his knee.

Ishanti got out of his car and went around the front of it, keeping both his hands in plain view, keeping his eyes on the prison, purposely not turning to see who was coming up on his right.

Skinny did not look at the yard but looked at Ishanti, remembering him clearly but more impressed with him now than he had been before, when they had met in the prison, Skinny something less than a rookie.

When Skinny got close, Ishanti said, "It just not the same." He turned and looked at Skinny, studying him, acknowledging his presence. "What they do now for exercise?"

Skinny did not reply right away but just kept on looking, his eyes alert but guarded.

"Aerobics," he replied finally.

Skinny held the Louisville Slugger on his shoulder, both hands gripping it as if he were ready to go up to bat. A moment later, he bent down and picked up a shell.

"They get those tapes with the instructions," he went on. "Put on their leotards with all the colors. . . ."

He threw the shell into the air, then hit it with the bat, watching critically as the shell whined away.

Ishanti did not say anything but waited to hear what would come next.

"Things change," Skinny said with a shrug, looking back before he looked down, searching for another shell to hit. "You used to be Big Jerome. Now you're Ishanti."

"Things change," Ishanti concurred. "But I still the same person—and things *never* change so much they in there doing aerobics."

Skinny smiled thinly before he bent down again.

"No," he agreed. "They don't change that much."

"Used to be," Ishanti went on, gesturing to the other side of the fence in a way that indicated the time they had spent inside together, "you got something to say, we meet and we talk. Didn't need no man with a rifle."

"*You* had him before," Skinny replied. "I figured it was my turn."

Skinny tossed the second shell in the air and swung at it, leaning into the effort; but midway through his swing, the bat stopped cold. There was a sharp slap of wood against flesh. When he figured out what had happened, he saw that Ishanti had simply reached out and grabbed the bat near the label, placing his huge hand where the shell should have hit.

"Don't need no stick you want to talk to me," Ishanti said, not releasing the bat. "Don't need no man with a rifle."

At first, Skinny was duly impressed, then very suddenly he was unreasonably angry. Ishanti was physically imposing, intimidating, and while he could deal with that fairly readily—his years as a policeman had taught him that, at least—he suddenly felt what Ruth had felt when she had been confronted by a hostile man of similar stature. He understood her fear. He felt the weakness in her knees and her heart in her chest. He felt the quivering, empty

feeling in her belly and the anger came right then, because he knew instinctively that something had been
taken away from her forever, a certain joy and carefree
lack of concern. He released the bat, allowing Ishanti to
have it, unzipped his jacket, and took out his gun, turning
slightly as he did so, holding it down along his leg, hidden
from view.

Ishanti did not look at Skinny but looked at the bat
before he casually tossed it off to one side.

"What do you want to talk to me about?" Ishanti asked.
"Not going to stay here all night."

Skinny brought the long, silver revolver up slowly,
keeping it low.

"I am not fucking around with you, Jerome. Do not
fuck around with me."

Ishanti looked from the revolver to Skinny, his eyes
moving slowly.

"You not going to shoot me," he predicted.

"I won't kill you," Skinny snapped in reply, at that
moment meaning it, "but I'll cripple you." He pointed
the revolver at Ishanti's right knee. "Count on it." He
flicked the barrel, indicating the bat near Ishanti's feet.
"You had a weapon." He flicked the barrel again, indicating Theriot in the guard tower. "I have a witness. Sounds
familiar, right? I pulled your file." In the burnt orange
light, Skinny's eyes appeared hot, almost feral. "You want
to play silly games, try to impress me some more, or you
want to talk?"

Ishanti seemed to consider that, as if he were weighing
the two options. He looked past Skinny, at the tent city
next to the prison, then back.

"*You* not the same man," he observed, his voice calm,
matter-of-fact. "Man I knew played it straight. Had to
respect him for that." When Skinny did not say anything,

he added, "I already asked you, what you want to talk to me about?"

Skinny relaxed his grip on his revolver, but just slightly.

"The Silver Lily," he began. "You own it?"

Ishanti seemed puzzled by that.

"Henry own it. I lease it, pay him a salary to run the bar—he gets paid twice."

"That's not what he says."

"Yeah?" Ishanti replied, his voice a dubious sneer. "What do he say?"

"He says you threatened to burn the place down unless he sold it to you—so he did."

Ishanti shook his head side to side almost sorrowfully.

"Henry afraid of his own shadow. I didn't have to threaten nothing. I offer him a deal, he take it—best deal he ever make. Now he see you come in, think there trouble, tell you a story to cover himself."

Skinny thought about that for a moment, realizing the disparity between the accounts was unimportant.

"What about Evans Charles? He worked for you, too."

"Worked for me, worked for everyone. Man available for what come along. Too bad he dead." Ishanti's black eyes fixed on Skinny's eyes in a challenging glare. "Got nothing to do with me."

"Yeah?" Skinny remarked, mimicking Ishanti's own dubious sneer. "How about Nickel? He got nothing to do with you either?"

Ishanti thought about that a while longer than he had his previous answer.

"Nickel work for me," he acknowledged finally. "Mainly do what I tell him, here and there."

"You tell him to beat the shit out of Ruth?" Skinny asked, his voice deceptively calm.

"Don't know no Ruth," Ishanti replied. "Never tell Nickel to beat up on nobody."

Skinny examined Ishanti's face as if he could see through to the truth—or at least catch some trace of a lie—but all he saw were his black, sloe eyes in his dark face and his broad, sloping brow. He allowed his revolver to fall back beside his leg.

"I'm looking for Dwayne Charles," Skinny said. "Evans Charles's son."

Ishanti nodded slightly, as if, finally, they had reached some point on which they could agree.

"Know him," he said. "Know he need to be found. Agnes dead, he got no place to go."

"You see him, you call me," Skinny added.

"I see him, I hold onto him," Ishanti replied. "Then I call you."

"That's even better," Skinny agreed.

Ishanti held Skinny's gaze for a long moment, then started to turn away toward his car.

"One more thing," Skinny went on.

Ishanti stopped and looked back.

"You tell Nickel I'm looking for him. Tell him to expect me."

Ishanti looked at Skinny speculatively, obviously appraising him and more than a little annoyed.

"You know better than that," he said. "Don't even want to hear it—you settle your personal business on your own time."

Skinny accepted that because he knew he was right, and as Ishanti got into his car, put his revolver back into its holster. He picked up his bat. He found a rock this time, not a shell, tossed it into the air, and hit it so hard it flew out of sight like a shot.

29

From the prison, Skinny did not go to the hospital to see Ruth, as he had planned, but went home before he went out again. He felt restless, unable to sit still. For a while, he just drove around aimlessly, then he found himself on the expressway, once again going over the Mississippi River Bridge. In Marrero, he went past the McDonald's and Brown's Lounge, past the Villa d'Ames and the Silver Lily, going slowly, checking things out, trying to decide what he should do, unaware that Dwayne saw him when he drove past—for Dwayne it had been a long afternoon.

After he had gotten himself into position beneath the Silver Lily and after he had eaten another can of Vienna sausage, Dwayne had found that he did not have anything to do. He had napped and he had run through his stock of readily available daydreams; but even then it was just early afternoon—and the waiting had begun to get on his nerves. He had found a place where there was clearance enough for him to roll over onto his back, and for almost two hours he had lain there, staring at the floorboards a foot overhead, all the while smelling the musty smell of the dirt all around him. He had heard Henry moving about, and from the footsteps he had tried to figure out where he was and what he was doing. Three times, other footsteps had joined Henry's, but Dwayne had figured out quickly that they were just deliverymen. He could hear the conversations quite clearly. About midafternoon, he worked his way back into the place he had made earlier and looked out, but nothing had changed except the position of the sun, though the clear view the bright light gave him convinced him he was right where he wanted to be.

Later on, Henry had turned on the jukebox, and Dwayne had liked that. He liked the old-fashioned music it played, the old recordings crackling and hissing, the voices and the instruments small and tinny but light and gay, seeming to come from the next room. He remembered that his mother often kept a radio on, and one song in particular made him think of her, the woman's voice so moving, filling him with an unfamiliar sadness and warmth. Soundlessly, he mouthed the words to the song, just as he had done in church the times his auntee had made him go, having only a vague idea what they meant and a half beat behind but liking the way they felt on his lips.

> *I can feel the night coming*
> *So hard and so fast*
> *It starts out so peaceful*
> *But it never lasts;*

The woman's voice was pure and clean, tinged with regret, standing out from the instruments behind it:

I had me a good man
So sweet and so strong
Yes, Lord, he was a fine man
But I treated him wrong;

I wanted a good time
And I thought I could play
'Til a silver-tongued devil
Led me astray;

The instruments took over then, a low murmuring of brass covered by a piano, the sounds easy, as if giving the woman solace, time to rethink her regret:

Now my man is gone
And my baby, too
I once had a rainbow
Now all I have is blue;

Then the woman's voice took off, soaring, even cleaner now but harder, too, edged and plaintive:

If you walk the high wire
One day you must fall
All your love will just leave you
Beyond recall.

The piano tapered off, an echo, the sound fading slowly. For a few moments the song filled Dwayne with a longing he did not understand, a gentle emotion; but shortly after the song ended Henry unplugged the jukebox, and the anger quickly returned in its place.

At sundown, Dwayne got into position and stayed there. At dusk, when he was certain he could not be seen, he wedged open the plywood, allowing him to look out, giving him a clear field of fire.

Just after dark, the first few patrons arrived. Henry had turned on the bright light over the Silver Lily's front door, and Dwayne could see each arrival plainly, the people, mostly men by themselves, lit up like a nighttime scene on TV. The light carried out into the parking area and beyond, to the street. Dwayne made his eyes follow the movements of his hands, aiming his vision, holding his father's gun steady on each customer who went through the door. He would never have seen Skinny except that Skinny was in his truck, the cab of the pickup high enough to be seen over the cars that were parked on the street. Less than ten minutes later, Nickel appeared.

Nickel had on a dark blue suit with gray pinstripes and a white shirt with an open collar, the collar arranged out over the lapels of the suit. Even at some distance Dwayne knew who he was—he was not big like Ishanti, but he was still big. As he walked between two parked cars, Nickel adjusted the suit coat by rolling his shoulders and rebuttoning the button. Dwayne kept the front sight blade centered on his chest, lining it up with the notch on the frame. He did not trust himself to cock the revolver but began to put pressure on the trigger, feeling the tension increase in the mainspring and seeing peripherally the hammer starting to roll back.

Suddenly, there were three shots in quick succession.

Then three more.

Dwayne's vision was limited by his own concentration, but he caught a glimpse of a white man, he was certain of it, behind Nickel before he began to fire, too, not wanting to miss his chance, pulling the trigger again and again, feeling the recoil, seeing the bright flash, surprised at how easy it seemed, for some reason very nearly sound-less and in slow motion, Nickel hit, falling back against the side of the car he had just passed, sliding down, his expression both stunned and obviously hurt. It took Dwayne a moment to realize when the revolver was empty, just clicking, the five cartridges expended. He had the presence of mind to remove the piece of brick that was holding open the plywood skirt, then he scrambled back the way he had planned, emerging on the far side of the Silver Lily, hearing nothing more than his ears ringing, starting to run back toward the levee, feeling no remorse whatsoever, only a strange sense of excitement and a gratification he did not really understand.

30

From Marrero, Skinny went home and stayed there, though for a while he was tempted to go back out to shoot pool. He wandered aimlessly around his apartment—just as he had wandered previously when he had been driving—pleased when finally he concluded that his wandering inside was a whole lot cheaper on gas. Along about that time, he went up to bed and went to sleep, aggravated more than a little when, some time later, he was awakened by a persistent pounding on his door.

"Hold on," he said irritably as he got out of bed, taking his silver gun with him. "What?" he asked loudly as he went down the stairs. "What?" he asked again even more loudly, genuinely surprised when William Dryden replied.

Out on the walkway, it was the special agent from the DEA, all right, his blue eyes hard as glass, without any trace of good humor; and right behind him was Skinny's own boss, Ted Grather, the acting chief of detectives, his expression somber and a little concerned.

"If you'd call before you came by," Skinny noted, looking at William Dryden, trying to read him, "you wouldn't always catch Skinny in his drawers."

"We'll wait while you get dressed," Ted Grather said, his tone neutral but still conveying the fact that for Skinny getting dressed was something more than a suggestion.

Skinny looked at them both, feeling an annoyed anger rising up to his cheeks, then without saying anything else he turned and went back upstairs, leaving the door open, leaving them to come in or stay out, whichever they wanted.

Skinny was irritated that they had shown up so dramatically in the middle of the night, but more than that, he knew, he was angry with himself, angry that he had overreacted when he had followed William Dryden into the government employees' parking garage.

Dumb, he said to himself as he put on jeans and a fresh shirt, remembering how he had thrown the special agent into the elevator then choked him with his own tie. *That was dumb.*

What he hadn't counted on was William Dryden being so petty about it, making a complaint and going to see his boss, Ted Grather.

You should have known, he chided himself, knowing, too, that *he* had been wrong.

He rinsed his face with cold water, brushed his teeth, wet his hands and ran them through his hair, combing it after a fashion; then he went downstairs, as prepared as he could be to take his medicine, hoping he would not get another suspension—but totally *un*prepared to see a third man methodically searching his apartment.

Skinny looked from William Dryden to Ted Grather, then watched the technician on his hands and knees checking under the furniture, kneading the carpet as he moved, his fingers probing, digging into the long, green pile.

"I have a warrant," William Dryden said, his voice crisp, unapologetic but without malice or satisfaction.

"He came to get me first," Ted Grather explained, "as a courtesy."

Ted Grather was a large man with a big face and closely cut gray hair. For almost six years, he had been the acting chief of detectives. Next to William Dryden, he seemed a very large man, though even in comparison it was obvious that William Dryden could hold his own—they were simply two different creatures, a city cop and a federal agent, as unlike as a shark and a bull.

Skinny was simply disconcerted.

As many times as he had seen searches conducted or had conducted them himself—and even though he knew there was nothing illegal in the apartment to find—still he was amazed at how intrusive it seemed, as if he were being publicly examined himself.

The technician spread the curtains between his hands, inspecting them closely, then took them by the hem and shook them until the heavy material billowed. Skinny looked away from the proceedings when he heard William Dryden and Ted Grather conferring. He heard Ted Grather say, "That won't be necessary," before he looked at Skinny. "He wants to read you your rights. I told him—"

"I heard what you told him," Skinny cut him off, a hard impatience in his tone. "Now you want to tell Skinny what this is all about?"

Ted Grather put his hands in his pockets and pursed his lips, not unsettled at all by Skinny's anger but deferring to William Dryden.

"Nickel was shot tonight," William Dryden said. "My man," William Dryden reminded him. "His name is Anthony Toin—he's a DEA *agent*."

"Yeah?" Skinny remarked. "So?" he added, pointedly allowing his lack of concern to show.

Behind his glasses, William Dryden's eyes were hot and cold at the same time, fiery, fiercely objective. He reached into the inside pocket of his suit jacket and came out with two separate sets of documents, one folded three times, one four. "This is your copy of the search warrant," he noted, and tossed the document aside, onto a chair. "This," he said, holding the second document by one end, offering it to Skinny, "is a copy of the report filed by the ATF agent who interviewed you initially, after you had reported the boat exploding and sinking."

Skinny took the copy of the report but did not look at it, waiting for William Dryden to go on.

"In that report, you accurately describe a limited production weapon Colt Industries proposed to the military, a small-caliber centerfire with a select firing capability—only a few were made, and a number of those were stolen."

"They were stolen from a storage facility in Maryland," Skinny observed, not sure where William Dryden was headed. "Gatzke told me."

The special agent glanced at Ted Grather, as if affirming that he had heard Skinny's remark, too.

"When I last saw you," he went on, his eyes back on Skinny, steady in a way that indicated he had *not* reported the entirety of that meeting, "you told me that you believed Agent Toin had beaten up your girlfriend."

"I don't just believe it," Skinny interjected. "I *know* it."

"Where were you earlier this evening?" William Dryden asked coolly. "Other than meeting with Ishanti?"

Skinny thought about that for a moment, again feeling a flush come into his cheeks, not surprised that the special agent knew about his meeting with Ishanti—for anyone who cared to follow, he had left a trail a mile wide. He decided not to answer the question, to let the special agent run out his line.

"The point is," William Dryden went on when it became apparent that Skinny was not going to reply, turning, addressing himself to Ted Grather as if Skinny weren't even there, "we have a motive, and we have confirmed access to a weapon, a rare weapon of the same sort that was used to shoot Agent Toin. If I can prove that he had the opportunity"—he waved his hand in Skinny's direction—"if he was anywhere in the vicinity of the Silver Lily when the shooting took place, I'm going to arrest him."

"Arrest me for what?" Skinny asked, not getting it, his voice loud and nasal and agitated.

William Dryden looked right at him before he replied, his cold blue eyes locked on Skinny's eyes.

"For the attempted murder of a federal agent."

Skinny was so surprised by that that for a moment he did not speak. He waved his arms as if he were getting ready, but no words came out.

The technician passed between William Dryden and him, on his way to search the small kitchen.

"That's quite a stretch, Dryden," he said finally, "because I wrinkled your necktie."

"You had the motive," the special agent countered, self-contained and composed. "You had access to the weapon. All I have to do is to put you at the scene." Again he turned to Ted Grather. "After we've finished searching for the weapon, we'll want to run a neutron activation test, to see whether or not he's fired a gun."

Ted Grather seemed to consider that, nodding thoughtfully, looking down, his hands still in his pockets.

"Maybe you better read him his rights," he finally agreed.

"You're a big help," Skinny noted.

"You'll be on paid leave," he added, "until this gets resolved."

"Jesus Christ," Skinny said, amazed at how quickly things were happening around him.

The technician continued his slow, thorough search and after a while came over to test Skinny's hands; and it was only then, after glaring in silence alternately at Ted Grather then at William Dryden, that Skinny truly realized the seriousness of his situation. He had, himself, arrested people with no more of a case than William Dryden already had against him. And if the special agent could verify what obviously he already suspected, that Skinny was at the scene, which he *had been*, passing by, Skinny's skinny ass was history.

Holy shit, he said to himself, feeling a thin, panicky fear creep into his thinking, an image involuntarily forming of being locked inside a prison without the key to get out.

31

From what he knew of Dwayne and of the boy's situation, Ishanti had surmised that he would be hiding out in either one of two places, either at his auntee's old shack or near where his father, Evans, had kept his boat. A boy of that age, Ishanti felt certain, would not go too far but would stay close to the places he knew. So after leaving Skinny and leaving behind the parish prison—and after stopping at the McDonald's on the way—he went first to Agnes's shack then farther on down the batture.

Even though it had been a few years since he had gone out by the river, still Ishanti found his way easily. That stretch was known to him—he had, after all, played in and around there just as Dwayne had, from the time he was old enough to walk and to get himself into trouble. He knew the soft spots to avoid and where the river sand made easy going. He knew the smells and the sounds of the water. The high quarter moon provided ample light, and after about a half hour, he found the old pier; and after that without much difficulty he found the narrow path that lead into the trees. Before too much longer he found the crude camp where Dwayne had been living.

In a small clearing, a heavy wooden box served as a chair. A large cardboard box made a shelter with a floor; in the box was a blanket. An old coat served as a pillow. Nearby were the remains of a fire and close to that was a hole he presumed was for trash disposal. In one way, Ishanti felt sorry for Dwayne, for how he had been living, but in another way, he knew it was not nearly as bad as it seemed: the boy in him understood such raw, unsupervised adventure. He sat on the wooden box and waited, listening to the soft sounds of night on the river, his mind blank but receptive, tempted by the hamburger and french fries he had brought out for Dwayne.

Although he had been born and raised in the violence-plagued housing project nearby, it wasn't until he was in prison that Ishanti had realized just how sheltered his life had actually been. His mother had protected him, providing him a home, and his life had been focused, on sports, on being a star. And while he had heard the stories and sometimes had even seen the hard evidence—the pools of blood on the ground, the hysterical victims—it wasn't until he had been locked up that he had witnessed first-hand man's own violent inhumanity to man. He had seen for himself the gang rapes, the stabbings, the brutal beatings administered by both inmates and guards, and forced to deal with that situation, he had realized fairly quickly how undeveloped, how childlike most men remained all their lives, carrying with them their small fears and concerns, wanting things as a child wants them, immediately, for their own instant gratification—he had seen one man stomped to death for a cube of green Jell-O. And what he had learned from that was to provide those supposedly grown-up men what it was they wanted most of all: answers without questions. Authority. The security of doing just what they were told. He had merely asserted himself, made his considerable presence known, and the result had been remarkable, an obedience that made longing for star status a thing of the past. What that had provided him was money, a certain knowledge of how the feeding chain worked, money enough to pay off the pardon board and to buy his way out. So in that way he had thrived in the prison. He had grown, mentally and physically; and when he had gotten out, he had carried on in that same vein, drawing people to him by knowing what they should do. He avoided drugs and the people who used them because drugs brought a skewed set of needs; women, too, could be confusing because very often they seemed to know inherently and without doubt what they wanted. But children were never a problem to him, because after he had learned to treat adults as children, he had learned just the opposite, to show children the respect due adults. So as he sat on that box in Dwayne's camp, Ishanti did not for one second believe he would have a problem with Dwayne. He did not even consider it—and a while later, he heard him. He heard the sound of his running, his sneakers slapping the ground, then when he got close, the wet, slurping sound the mud made when, obviously, he took a wrong step.

When Dwayne appeared at the edge of the clearing, Ishanti said quietly, "I here. Don't want to spook you. This Ishanti."

Dwayne froze right where he was.

"Brought you some dinner," Ishanti went on. "Thought you could use it."

Dwayne was more than a little startled, the excitement he had felt a moment before immediately transforming, becoming a quick fear mixed with dread.

"How long you been here?" he asked.

Ishanti thought that a curious question for Dwayne to ask first—a thought that would come back to him later.

"Been here awhile," Ishanti replied. "Been listening to the river, how nice it sound, like it telling you secrets." He started to stand up, but as soon as he did, Dwayne took a step back. He reached out, never quite standing, and put the white paper sack on the ground between them, then shifted his weight back down onto the box.

Only then did Dwayne think of the box, angry with himself that he hadn't bothered to rebury it when he had meant to. He wondered if Ishanti would steal the guns and the money inside it.

"You okay here until it start to rain," Ishanti observed, looking around, then allowing his eyes to drift back to Dwayne. "Rain or get cold." He dropped his gaze to the sack he had put on the ground. "You not too hungry," he added, "okay I eat your fries?"

That caught Dwayne in a dilemma. He *was* hungry, but he did not want to accept the food from Ishanti.

Ishanti retrieved the sack, took out the french fries, put the sack back on the ground.

"Used to," Ishanti began, casually munching on the fries as he spoke, "when I your age, I come out here, too, me and my friends. Sometimes, we catch a log going by, float with it, catch the current, and go down as far as the zoo." He waved a french fry at the bridge in the distance. "Scared the shit outta me, never did know how to swim."

Just for a moment, involuntarily, Dwayne caught a glimpse of the muddy brown water before he had jumped into it, rippled and swirling around the badly damaged boat. He felt his fear of the water, then immediately he thought of his father in the cabin as the boat had slipped beneath the surface, stern-first—his father had been afraid of the water, too.

"I sorry about your auntee," Ishanti went on, correctly reading the shift in Dwayne. "She a fine person, know you miss her."

"Don't matter," Dwayne replied right away. Suddenly, he felt the weight of the revolver tucked in the waistband of his jeans, though now he was afraid of it, afraid of its being found. "Did you kill my daddy?" he asked.

"No," Ishanti replied, "and don't know who did—don't know who meant the man harm."

"You going to find out?" Dwayne asked.

Ishanti thought about that for a moment, wondering how it felt to have a father about whom you cared. His own father had walked off before he was born.

"Could," he replied. "Could if you want me to—but that not going to bring him back."

"He went down on the boat," Dwayne said.

"Heard that," Ishanti replied, feeling an unfamiliar emotion inside him, a feeling he was not accustomed to.

"I there when my auntee was killed," Dwayne went on. "She told me to run. Made me. I go down the posts under her house, get away, heard the shots." He tugged at the sleeve on his T-shirt. "Shouldn't have left her."

"You right to do what she tell you," Ishanti corrected him, not knowing quite what else to say. There was something about Dwayne that reminded him of himself at the same age, some combination of independence and uncertainty and loneliness. "Eat your dinner," he said, gesturing at the sack, " 'fore I eat it for you."

Dwayne hesitated, then stepped forward and picked up the sack. When Ishanti held out the french fries, he hesitated again before he finally took them, moved away to the edge of the clearing, sat down, and began to eat hungrily.

Ishanti stayed where he was, watching Dwayne wolf down the food, surprised at how old he felt next to him, surprised at how much of being a boy was still inside him. It didn't seem that long ago that he had been playing on the batture himself, poking around through the junk that washed up, hiding out in his own secret place, taking a pole and trying to catch catfish. What separated him from Dwayne, he realized a few moments later, wasn't nearly so much the years or the state of mind as it was the knowing, knowing what would come next, the learning about girls, learning to drive, going out on your own.

Going out on your own, Ishanti thought, *whether you want to or not*.

His mother had died while he had been in the prison, and the day of her funeral had been the hardest day of his life—a day he recalled very clearly.

He had been in his bunk when the guards had come to get him. They had asked him not to make any trouble. So he had gone along with them, still in those days walking his cool walk, one arm held rigid at his side, working his way forward around it, nodding and signing to his friends as he passed. The guards had escorted him to a lock-down cell, and although he had been surprised about that, sure they were wrong, he had entered without complaining, settling into the small space, knowing someone would be along to tell him the reason. Not too much later, he had seen the prison chaplain approach, and he had known intuitively what had happened.

"Your mother died this morning," the chaplain had told him. He remembered that the chaplain's skin was a pale, pasty white. "She had a heart attack and went very quickly." His eyes were soft blue and watery, his voice curt. "You'll be kept locked down until the day after the funeral. That's the policy. I'm sorry."

"When's the funeral?" he had asked.

"Day after tomorrow," he had been told.

From the lock-down cell, if he looked up, through the tier high above, during the day he had been able to see a small square of sky; and what he remembered most about his time in that cell was how blue that square had appeared, how clear and seemingly endless. He remembered the anger he had felt, the sense of unfairness, the sadness. But looking at that square of sky stood out in his mind because it seemed after a while to be like looking down, directions confused, inside himself at the vast emptiness there. He remembered the day of the funeral, reading the notice in the newspaper the guard brought him, knowing with certainty that he was all on his own. He remembered the huge doubt that had brought, and watching Dwayne now, finishing up the last of the hamburger, gobbling the rest of the fries, he knew that self-doubt was far too strong for a boy to bear by himself.

"You finish," he said, "you come with me for a while. Come back here later."

Dwayne slowed his chewing appreciably, uncertain what he should do; but after a quick, furtive glance at Ishanti, his dark shape as big as the side of a freighter, he realized there wasn't much he *could* do.

"Got to pee first," he said, and got to his feet. He wadded the paper sack into a ball. Ishanti did not say anything, so he trotted out of the clearing toward the river, taking the revolver out of his waistband as he did so. From the water's edge, he threw the gun into the river, checked his pockets, and threw the spare bullets, too, relieved when neither the gun nor the bullets made much of a splash, relieved to be rid of them. When he started back, away from the river, he was only a bit startled to discover that Ishanti was not too far behind him, waiting in the low weeds.

Dwayne slowed to a walk and together he and Ishanti went to the top of the levee, not hiding, walking in plain view. Shortly thereafter, Dwayne felt Ishanti reach down and take his hand in his. Dwayne was amazed at how big Ishanti's hand was, and he was amazed that Ishanti did not hold him tightly or seem to want to keep him from jerking away but just seemed to guide him, to keep him from missing a step.

32

Ishanti and Dwayne went down the levee, following the slow turn in the river, past Agnes's shack, before they went down and got into Ishanti's car. Even at some distance they had seen the crowd that had gathered in front of the Silver Lily, and they had seen the police cars, so Ishanti drove off in the opposite direction. A while later he stopped to use a pay phone, and a while after that he stopped one street over from the Silver Lily, directly behind it but in the next block.

"Called Henry," Ishanti explained to Dwayne.

Dwayne again felt the quick fear, the foreboding that his part in the shooting was about to be discovered.

"He going to meet us," Ishanti continued, "tell us what going on at the Lily—when he get here you get in the backseat."

Dwayne fought back the urge to run, to throw open the car door and to run as fast as he could. He knew that Ishanti would catch him. He made himself sit quietly, but with a fingernail he scraped anxiously at the side of his thumb. His feet moved up and down.

Ishanti played a tape while they waited, a saxophone

that seemed like smooth light in the dark, music of a sort Dwayne had never heard before. The thick carpet in the car and the soft leather seats were luxurious, a stark contrast to his cardboard box on the river.

It was nearly an hour before Henry appeared, his broad, round shape unmistakable, his short, fat legs seeming to roll him side to side as much as forward. When Dwayne saw him, he twisted around and slid into the backseat headfirst.

"Next time," Ishanti said evenly, not irritated but giving an order, "you get out one door and get back in the other."

Henry saw the car and got into it, breathing heavily, as if the sixty-yard walk had been an exertion.

"Nickel shot," he said without being asked what had happened. "Shot two, maybe three times in front the Lily, when he about to come in. He hurt bad."

To Dwayne it seemed Ishanti remained surprisingly calm.

"The bar mostly empty," Henry went on. "It early. I hear the shots, call the police 'fore I go out. See Nickel down. Shot here and here." Henry touched himself on the shoulder and the side of his chest.

The *right* side, Dwayne noted, the side that had been away from him, feeling a roller coaster of elation and disappointment.

"Maybe shot more. Hard to tell with all the blood. His chest making a sucking noise when he breathe, got a big hole in it." Henry touched his own chest again, in front. "Covered it up with a bar rag—that all I had. Police come, say I did the right thing. Got to get back. They still there. I supposed to be taking a leak."

Ishanti had looked at Henry when he had first gotten into the car, but then he had looked away and settled back in his seat, his eyes steady but distant. He nodded, indicating that Henry could leave if he wanted.

"I call you," Henry added. "Leave a message when the police gone."

Ishanti nodded again.

Henry was put off by Ishanti's lack of response, put off and apprehensive, but he didn't have time to consider it right then, not if he wanted to stay out of trouble with the police. After a moment, he got out of the car. He was about to shut the door behind him when he saw the back door open; and it was only then that he saw Dwayne.

Dwayne got out and shut the back door, got in the front, pulled that door shut, too, moving right past Henry without acknowledging him in any way at all. When Henry stared at him, taken by surprise, trying to put Ishanti and him together in his mind, wondering what it meant, Dwayne stared right back at him malevolently, willing him away, a black look that frightened Henry as much as the gun had.

Dwayne watched as Henry walked away, glancing back before he disappeared around the rear corner of the Silver Lily.

For a while, Ishanti did not move at all but remained very still, appearing deceptively relaxed, his fingers lightly touching the steering wheel. He had met Nickel in the prison and knew him to be a violent man, with a temper. He and Nickel got along only because Nickel was afraid of him, afraid to challenge him directly, though once or twice, he knew, Nickel had worked against him, behind his back. He had allowed Nickel to continue to work for him because he was good at maintaining order in the clubs. In his own way, he was reliable and predictable. He was good at making collections. While it did not surprise Ishanti that Nickel had met with violence—and while certainly there was no love lost between them—still Ishanti knew he could not just let the attack go. If he did, every cowboy from Westwego to Greata would declare open season on his clubs.

Dwayne was unsettled by Ishanti's lack of response, and when Ishanti started the car without saying another word, he decided to do something about it.

"Was around earlier," he began.

Ishanti said nothing.

"Tall, skinny white man," Dwayne went on. "He the one pulled me out the river."

Ishanti seemed to be listening.

"He a policeman."

"Didn't know that," Ishanti remarked, then clarified what he had meant. "Didn't know he the one had pulled you out the river."

Dwayne nodded.

"Seen him around earlier."

"Seen him around where?"

"In his truck," Dwayne replied, pleased that he had gotten Ishanti's attention but a little hesitant now that he had it. "He drive by the Silver Lily."

"Before Nickel was shot?"

Dwayne nodded, not liking the tone he had heard in Ishanti's voice, correctly tuned in to his thoughts and picking up the spark of anger.

"You sure?"

Dwayne nodded again.

"Damn," Ishanti said softly, putting that together with what he had already been told. "Damn," he said again, his thoughts disordered, tinged with some something he could not quite identify.

He knew he could not tolerate a bad cop. He couldn't. They were too unpredictable. The cops who played it straight were difficult enough; a cop gone bad was a wild card there was no predicting at all. And wasn't it more than a little curious that Skinny had been near the boat when it exploded, near enough to rescue Dwayne? And he *had* threatened Nickel, there was no doubt about that. Now Nickel had been shot, and there was a witness to put him in the area.

"Damn," Ishanti said yet again, angry that he could not accept what was readily apparent.

So why had Skinny *told* him he was out after Nickel? Why had he pulled the boy out of the river?

Ishanti put the car in gear and drove away, away from the river. He had questions that he could not quite put into words, and that made him angrier still because in a way it would be so much simpler if he did not know the one thing about which he *was* certain: events were not always quite what they appeared—he had paid for that little piece of knowledge with the years he had spent in the prison. He wanted confirmation, something more than a circumstantial sequence.

At an intersection he slowed, groping for the name Skinny had mentioned, then he sped up again.

Ruth. That was it. The girlfriend.

He could ask her.

33

In a replay of the way he had started out the previous day, first thing the next morning Skinny went to the hospital to see Ruth. Since he didn't have to go to work and time wasn't a problem, on the way he stopped off to get pastries and two cartons of milk to take with him. By the time he arrived, the hospital was already well into its morning routine. Nurses were dispensing medication and catching up on paperwork. Doctors were making their rounds. Patients in wheelchairs and on gurneys were being wheeled about, taken to various places. Skinny ate a lemon Danish as he rode up in the elevator, curious to see which set of doors, front or back, would open when he arrived at Ruth's floor, disappointed when the same set of doors opened at each stop on the way. He started to lick the sugar from his fingers, thought of the germs that were undoubtedly around him, wiped his fingers on his jeans instead.

Ruth had awakened some time before, it seemed, because she had had time enough not only to get up and get dressed but also to go back to sleep. When Skinny looked in the door, she was sitting up in a chair, her hair neatly brushed, a new, smaller bandage in place across her nose, her chin on her chest as she slept, her lips slightly parted. After considering his options, Skinny got up on the bed and stretched out, looking past his boots at Ruth, all in all gratified by what he saw. The bruises on her face were fading, and she had her color back, the look of improving health. While no one would call her beautiful—her face was too long and too square, her cheekbones too roundly prominent—there was about her even at rest a certain energy. He was anxious to run the latest events past her, to learn what she thought, but he was not so anxious that he would wake her, particularly since he had all day. So he just waited, finally dozing himself, unaware that, when Ruth did wake up, she looked at him for an unusually long time without saying anything, her gaze expressing a range of discordant emotions, uncertainty, concern, hurt, and anger.

Finally, she said, "You look comfortable," to get his attention.

"I am," Skinny acknowledged, immediately opening his eyes, with both hands reaching behind his head to fluff up the pillows. "I brought pastries," he added, yawning then jerking his chin to indicate the paper sack he had left on the adjustable bedside table.

Ruth used the pastries as an excuse to let her eyes wander, not yet certain what to say. Earlier that morning, just about sunup, just after the nurse had come in to take her temperature, Agent Gatzke had come by, ostensibly looking for Skinny. But after Gatzke had told her what he wanted Skinny for, Ruth had realized that what he really wanted was to leave a message, not to see him, which was why he had come to see her. And in giving her the message, saying that he was sorry about his report, sorry that it was being used against Skinny, he had given her the details of the evening before, how Nickel had been shot and Skinny was the number-one suspect, a situation she could scarcely believe—a response Skinny read even then in her eyes.

"There's milk in there, too," he added, studying her, wanting her to speak first, feeling his own anger rise because he needed her just then, and once again, it seemed, she wasn't trusting him. He got up, went to the window, and looked out, careful not to say anything he might regret later.

Ruth felt Skinny move as much as she saw him, and she felt the shift in him, though still she did not know what to say. This was all so new to her, this kind of life where people tried to and did kill each other—and beat the tar out of someone to get the answer to a question. It was frightening and somehow sordid, and while she knew that she cared for Skinny a great deal, even loved him, she wasn't sure at all that this was a life she could share. And that was her choice, wasn't it, share it or leave it because it was so much a part of him? She saw that now in him as he looked out the window. She saw his short, slightly curved nose, the curving arch of his eyebrow, the angular line to his jaw. She saw the hard, unblinking cast to his eyes, the characteristic tension in his features, the way he was always focused, straight ahead—which often enough she had found flattering, mistaking it for fascination with *her*. At that moment again he put her in mind of a bird, but not a snowy egret this time, arms flapping as he hurried down into the water, but of a hawk, perhaps, or an owl, some sort of predator, a hunter, obeying his instincts, attacking straight ahead because that was what he knew how to do. For him there was no such thing as standing still, no such thing as a defensive posture, and to ask him to change would be to change the other parts, too: his rock-steady, unquestioning self-assurance, the un-self-consciousness and directness that allowed him to be what he was. For a moment she wondered why she hadn't seen it before. But how could she? she answered herself. How could she have seen what she didn't even know existed, a world as brutal as any in nature? Ruth felt a sorrow creep into her thoughts, a certain understanding.

From the window, Skinny said pointedly, "Don't you even want to ask Skinny whether or not he did it?"

"No," Ruth replied quietly because she had heard in his question the way he had reverted to the use of third person. She knew what that meant.

Skinny examined her face. She could feel it.

"I thought about it," he said, more to himself than to her. "I thought about shooting the son of a bitch. I'll admit that." He leaned back against the large pane of glass, looking in. "But Skinny does not ambush people. If he'd gone after Nickel, he would have walked right up to him and nailed him. Nickel would have known who he was."

Before he went on, he ran his hand over his face.

"I was hoping you'd help me, Ruth, help me piece it together. I don't know who told you what—"

"Agent Gatzke came by," Ruth interjected. "He's sorry his report is being used against you."

Skinny waved that away as unimportant.

"Don't you think you should at least talk to me, too? See what I have to say?"

"Yes," Ruth replied, meaning it, knowing she owed him that much and more, about to add, "I want to," but when she looked up and looked at him directly, she saw in his expression the same cold, controlled anger that she had seen once before in this same hospital room.

"You don't have to hurt him," she had said the same

day that she had been beaten. She had taken her hand away from his and used it to indicate her still-swelling face. "Not for this."

"I know I don't *have* to," he had replied.

And that said what? she wondered then. That he *wanted* to. He wanted to have his revenge, a conclusion that momentarily kept her from saying anything else—a long pause that Skinny interpreted as the rest of her answer.

"You're too hung up in yourself, Ruth," he went on, "too busy worrying about what *might* come next to allow yourself to see what's happening right now." His tone was hard, responding to his hurt and surprise, and matched his steady, unwavering gaze. "And you know what I think? I think you're taking your problems about maintaining a long-term relationship and putting them off on me. I think at some level you're doing it on purpose because you don't have the courage to work through your doubts."

Ruth did not reply to that, could not reply to that, because too many emotions swirled up in her at once. She was afraid of losing Skinny and she was afraid of remaining close, too. She was wary of words that predicated her actions yet she was not at all sure he wasn't right. However he had arrived there, Skinny had struck where she was most vulnerable, at the place where she didn't know answers herself.

"And I'm in a trick, Ruth. I don't have time for this right now. For the first time since I've known you, I need to come first—sometimes, you just have to run off your batteries, whether they're charged up or not."

Ruth knew what he was saying and knew about this he was right without question. She could sort through her own problems later. But before she could say anything, there was a knock at the door and immediately thereafter her doctor came in, not bothering to ask whether he should come back—an interruption Skinny was not prepared to tolerate.

"I'll come back," he said, stepping past Ruth and past the doctor, going out the door.

Ruth felt the doctor's hands on her jaw then his fingers gently pinching the bridge of her nose.

"I'm ready to go home," she said as he continued to examine her.

The doctor smiled paternally, benevolently, as if he were in the presence of a less-than-bright child.

"That's always a good sign," he said.

34

Skinny was learning, that much was for certain. He was learning that, for all the years he had been a policeman, he had never really understood the law, its power. He had known about it, of course, but the knowing had only been intellectual, without real feeling. He had known yet not known what it meant that your whole life could be taken from you, your basic rights and your freedom called into question for what it only *appeared* you had done. He was learning about the sort of fear that brought, not the up-the-spine chill he was familiar with, the adrenaline rush, but a fear like a weight pressing down on you, a slightly sick feeling in the pit of your stomach. And along with that he was learning about balance, about what it meant when you trusted someone who did not trust you in return. He was learning about lopsided affection. He had thought that the lack of trust was Ruth's problem alone, but he could see now that it was his problem, too. It seemed to him that, for his emotional investment, he was getting very little back in return.

Skinny knew that gunshot victims were almost invariably rushed to Charity Hospital, then when their condition was stable—and if they had the proper insurance—they were transferred to someplace a bit more humane. In the course of his work, it wasn't unusual for him to have to go to Charity Hospital fairly often, and as a result he knew people there who would tell him where he could find Nickel. If Nickel was in any kind of shape to talk, he *did* want to talk to him, to find out what he knew of what had happened. So after he left Ruth at the hospital on Napoleon, he drove downtown, going up St. Charles Avenue, around Lee's Circle, deliberately passing the DEA office at 1001 Howard and the government employees' parking garage, reminding himself of how he had overreacted, how he had very nearly beaten up a DEA special agent, knowing that within that response to Ruth's beating was the reason he was in such a jam.

Although it was only a few blocks from the Superdome and the elegant, beautifully maintained tower buildings along the Poydras Street corridor, Charity Hospital was in a bleak part of downtown, an urban backwater made up primarily of other hospitals and the low-rent businesses between and around them. The squat, blocky hospitals rose straight up from the sidewalks, diminishing pedestrians, making them feel out of place, and across the front of every store—the discount shoe and tie store, the store for prosthetic devices, the we-fill-welfare-prescriptions drugstore—there were steel bars protecting the glass that was, without exception, chipped, cracked, or broken. Nearby was the underside of an elevated expressway. Skinny drove up and over the two-lane wide ramp that lead to the entrance, parked between two ambulances near the exit, put a police light on the dash of his truck before he walked back, and went into Charity Hospital's huge emergency room.

No matter how many times he walked through the sliding glass doors, each time he did it Skinny felt somehow unprepared, not quite ready to encounter the apparent chaos and even more apparent apathy within. To the left of the doors, the large waiting area was full. Every seat was taken; a dozen or so people sat on the floor. Young doctors in green scrubs, older nurses in white, technicians, and assistants all moved with purpose, never stopping or looking around, avoiding eye contact and the inevitable question, how much longer do I have to wait? Across from the waiting area there was a long row of tables, each one surrounded by a white curtain hung from a shiny metal rail, and Skinny went down the row, looking for someone he knew—the tables, it seemed, were just another waiting area, a place for people too weak to sit up. On one table, a young woman, recently dead Skinny judged by her color, was lying face up unattended, her book bag on the floor nearby. On another table, an old man was gasping for breath. Skinny saw no one he knew, so he went across the waiting area and through the inner set of doors into the maze of examination rooms.

The corridors connecting the examination rooms were too narrow, crammed with gurneys and wheelchairs and portable equipment. Activity was nonstop and deliberate yet without apparent reason or rhyme. This, Skinny knew, was not a particularly busy time, nothing like a bad Saturday night or the night of a full moon, but still the comings and goings were too numerous to keep track of. There was the sense of a place under siege. He ducked into a shallow alcove and waited, knowing that, sooner or later, someone he knew would come into view.

Within a few minutes he saw an orderly who looked familiar, but right behind him he saw a nurse he knew a bit better. Though he couldn't remember with what, exactly, he recalled that she had helped him before. He started after her, bumped into a plastic bag of something hung on a thin metal pole, caught it before it fell, but lost the nurse around a corner. When he caught sight of her again, she was in the nurses' station, sorting through a tall stack of folders. Skinny went and stood where it seemed likely she would come out, but when she found the folder she was looking for, she turned and went out the other side.

Skinny cut through the same way she had and fell into step beside her, surprised at how fast she went.

"Remember me?" he asked, watching her and watching out for obstacles.

The nurse was in her fifties, he guessed, gray-haired and no-nonsense, the sort of woman who ran a tight ship and took pride in her gruffness.

"Yes," she replied, right to the point. "I haven't got time at the moment." She waved the folder at the examination rooms. "Find one that's empty and wait."

Skinny kept up with her only long enough to read the name on her name tag, then fell off her pace.

He looked up and down the corridor, saw one door that was open and went there, not noticing at first anything more than the fact that the bottom half of the examination table was vacant. When he stepped into the room, however, he saw the nurse who had been hidden by the open, extrawide door, and suddenly he noticed a whole lot at once.

The nurse was leaning across the other end of the examination table, her attention fixed on an instrument attached to the wall, and beneath her white uniform Skinny couldn't help noticing the line of her panties accenting her hips, and beneath that the white stockings over slim, muscular legs. When she reached out to reset the instrument, the hem of her uniform slid up several inches farther and Skinny heard the faint rustle of cotton sliding past nylon, a sound and a movement that brought his attention to the shadow he could sense farther up in the warm, white half-light between her thighs—all of which surprised him very pleasantly.

"Who are you?" he asked.

When she glanced at him, he saw that she was younger than he was, though not that much younger, maybe twenty-six or twenty-seven; and when she turned away from the wall, standing up rather than leaning, he realized she was only about five three or four, at most up to his chin. Her black hair was straight and fell well past her shoulders. Her eyes were warm brown and deep but easy to read.

"That's supposed to be my question," she said.

"This is Skinny," Skinny said automatically. "Nurse Brannan told me to wait."

"Then you better," this nurse replied.

She glanced around the examination room, checking that all was in order, and Skinny glanced at her name tag, noting both her name, Kim Espy, and the significant swell of her breasts, briefly wondering why such a plain, austere uniform, when worn by the right woman, could be so ridiculously sexy.

"Do you have your chart?" she asked.

"No," Skinny replied. "I'm here on business."

For a moment her gaze held his, and Skinny felt a catch in his chest, an excitement. He could see the fun in her eyes, the curious speculation. Her lips were both pliable and sensual. He'd bet she was quick to smile when she wanted to, quick to laugh—and he'd bet she'd cry at sad movies.

"There was a federal agent brought in last night," he went on. "He'd been shot. His name is Anthony Toin. I need to talk to him."

"And to talk to him you need to know where he is."

"Right," Skinny affirmed, noting the questioning look that came into her eyes, liking that, too. "I'm a policeman," he added.

"You don't look like a policeman," she remarked, "not any policeman I've ever seen."

"Skinny's Skinny," he replied. "That's what makes him different."

Nurse Espy smiled, more to herself than at him.

"I'll see what I can find out," she said. "Don't go away."

"I'll stay right here," Skinny said, watching her go, once again admiring the way she looked from the rear.

He leaned back against the examination table and crossed his arms on his chest, pleased by his good fortune, for a moment feeling all right, okay about himself, the weight of his worry lifted briefly. Nurse Espy was giving him a boost when he needed it, which was very different from Ruth, who when he needed her most was only compounding his problems. Ruth was high maintenance, he knew that, but just then he asked himself what it would be like if a woman maintained him instead—the fact that Nurse Espy looked so good in her uniform made the possibility even more attractive. Idly he allowed himself to picture what she would look like coming out of that uniform, in his mind's eye unzipping the long white zipper in back, splitting it off her, the contrast between that plain white dress and the lush skin beneath more than a little erotic. First he had her in a white bra and panties, very nurselike, then in something a little more elaborate, with lace like a fancy wrapping and a soft, slippery feel.

The straps came down off her shoulders. The stockings unsnapped, and there were other snaps, too. Skinny got so involved in various images of her he felt a little embarrassed when she finally came back—but not so embarrassed that he didn't for a second or two overlay his last image over her presence.

He looked up and smiled, a smile she returned with a mischievous look, as if she had been reading his mind.

"Tulane Medical Center ICU," she said. "Fifth floor. Across the street," she added, and pointed. "Nurse Brannan is right behind me. Got to go."

"Thanks," Skinny said, meaning it several ways at once.

"See you," she said. "Come by any time."

Skinny did not reply to that but watched her go, and after a moment went to the door himself and looked out. Nurses Brannan and Espy were down the hall to his right, so he slipped out to the left, catching the smile Nurse Espy shot him, tucking it away among his other images of her, something, possibly, to be considered again later.

35

Tulane Medical Center was a private hospital, considerably smaller than Charity, and although it was only across the street, for the difference in the feel of the place it might as well have been on another planet. The waiting area was small, clean, and uncrowded, and above the upholstered chairs with arms there was a color TV. On the floors there was carpet. The corridors were wide and uncluttered.

Following the neatly lettered signs, Skinny went up to the fifth floor and pushed through the double doors into the intensive care unit. Nine private rooms made up three sides of a square formed around a large, central station. Large windows in the walls gave a view into each room. As near as Skinny could tell, four rooms were vacant, five were in use, there were two nurses on duty. Anthony Toin was in the second room on the right, and Skinny just went on in, surprising both the patient and the uniformed policeman ostensibly there to protect him—both of whom were watching game-show TV.

"To hear Dryden tell it—" Skinny began.

"Hey, buddy," the policeman started, coming up out

of his chair, but he knew Skinny, by sight at least, and his alarmed anger settled.

"—you're at death's door."

"The man like to overstate things," Nickel replied, his tone and his expression impassive but belied by his heartbeat, which was displayed on a monitor over his head. Orange-yellow lines on an orange background took a leap. "How did you find me?"

"Lucky guess," Skinny replied. "Just to get it straight," he went on, "I didn't shoot you."

"I never said you did," Nickel hedged. "I never seen nothing."

"If it had been Skinny," Skinny assured him, "you'd have seen him. He'd have been right up in your face—and you wouldn't be waiting for the afternoon movie."

Nickel rolled his head to the left, apparently unconvinced—or unconcerned—and looked at the TV.

"Two people shot me," he said. "One on each side." He looked back at Skinny. "They dug two kinds of bullets out of me—if it was you, you got a friend."

Skinny thought about that for a moment, not sure what to make of it.

"Sorry about your girlfriend," Nickel went on. "I hope she's not hurt too bad." His eyes shifted to the uniformed policeman. "You go on, find yourself a cup of coffee somewhere, come back after while."

"I'm supposed to stay here," the young policeman said lamely, aware that he had already screwed up.

"If the man wanted to shoot me," Nickel replied, pointing out the obvious, "he'd already have done it—shot you, too, probably, make you wish you never had turned on the TV."

The policeman hesitated, his lips pressed tightly together, as if he really did have a choice whether or not to leave—which he didn't, Nickel had just told him, not if he wanted his lapse of attention to go unmentioned.

"I'll watch your hat," Skinny offered, adding his encouragement, wanting Nickel to talk and understanding there was a better chance if there wasn't a witness.

The young man left, giving both Nickel and Skinny a hard look, his anger apparent. Skinny stepped farther into the room, shut the door, and leaned back against it.

"I didn't want to hurt your girlfriend," Nickel went on. "Had to." He rearranged himself on the bed, as much as the tubes running into his arms would allow, grimacing as he did so then looking right at Skinny from his new, more upright position. The lines on the heart monitor flared again, though from the exertion or from what he was saying it was impossible to tell. "I had one of Ishanti's men with me when we found her. I had to make the man believe she didn't know where the boy was. I had to make it look good, otherwise he was going to want to take her."

"Take her where?" Skinny asked, not sold on the reason Nickel was giving for beating up Ruth.

"Take her to Ishanti, probably," Nickel replied.

Skinny was not sold on Nickel's expression either, the just-business look he was trying to maintain.

"I slapped her around some," he went on, "held her throat tight to keep her from talking—probably saved her life 'cause I did it."

Skinny felt a jolt of anger he found hard to control, a response from deep in his gut. He had seen the damage to Ruth's face, and he could picture all too well what had happened: Ruth wanting to scream, trying to, not even realizing that she couldn't. What he wanted to do was to start in on Nickel, slap *him* around some, make him feel the terror he knew Ruth had felt; but he didn't, for him a response so unnatural he had to give himself something to do. He stepped up to the bed and looked at Nickel's arms, the long, parallel scratches on his left hand and forearm confirming what he was saying.

"She's a fighter," Nickel added, looking at the scratches himself before he looked back at Skinny. "Full of fire for a white woman."

Skinny did not acknowledge that in any way at all but forced himself to keep going.

"When did Ishanti tell you to find the boy?" he asked, his voice curt.

"He didn't have to tell me," Nickel replied. "I just did it." His look changed to impatience, as if he were going over something so apparent it shouldn't have to be explained. "I knew Ishanti was good for blowing up the boat. When I heard the boy lived, I figured I better get to him first."

"You *know* Ishanti blew up the boat?" Skinny asked, the force of his anger going into an overstated expression of surprise.

"I don't *know* it," Nickel replied, his impatience near scorn. "I know he's *good* for it."

That's not the same thing, Skinny thought immediately, thinking of himself first, of his situation, then thinking of Ishanti, but not saying anything about either. All along everyone had assumed Ishanti was *good for* blowing up the boat, which undoubtedly he was, but that didn't necessarily mean that he had—a distinction that brought Skinny to a different, determined kind of anger, because he knew then where the mistakes had begun to be made.

"When Agnes was killed," Nickel went on, "the boy was lucky again, made off. I started looking for him—saw you that night, there in the Lily."

"Right," Skinny affirmed, remembering the feeling he

had had when he had gone into the Silver Lily that evening, when all activity had stopped; and remembering, too, the conversation with Ruth he had had later on, feeling so knowing, explaining to her about life in the projects.

"I followed you thinking maybe you had the boy or knew what had been done with him, stopped at the bridge."

"Why did you stop at the bridge?"

"They're too many police there, and no way off once you're on it. I knew you'd made me, figured you might be about to flag down a patrol car. I turned around and went back to the Lily. Next day, I found your girlfriend and asked her about the boy but didn't let her talk, made it look good, kept my cover."

Kept your cover, Skinny thought, again thinking of Ruth, of finding her in the alley, for some reason catching an image of the filth on her knees.

"I kept looking," Nickel went on. "Talked to Ishanti. Like he is, he didn't say anything. Then Dryden called me in, talked to me. He said to stay away from civilians, said to watch out for you. I knew what had happened."

"So why didn't you just call me?" Skinny asked, his voice so plaintive and angry Nickel looked at him strangely.

"That's not the way to do it," Nickel replied, "to call you. It brings too much heat on to go to the local police."

"Jesus," Skinny said almost involuntarily, not even beginning to know how to convey to Nickel all he was thinking. He saw the many mistakes that had been made, the pain needlessly inflicted, and he knew Nickel wouldn't hear him, not if he just said it, because the man couldn't even recognize his own inconsistencies, how his motives were all skewed about.

He started to say something anyway but ran his hand over his face instead, then went to the wall near the window and pretended to examine a piece of electronic equipment. He could feel Nickel's gaze on his back, but he just let him look. After a while, he picked up the uniformed policeman's hat from the table and idly regarded the badge affixed to the front.

It was a hazard of working undercover, Skinny knew, that you could get so caught up in your role that you lost sight of your purpose. If you stayed with it too long, it began to seem that the purpose *was* to maintain the role, to actually become what you were trying so hard to appear to be. He had seen it before, in himself and in others, the very real danger: undercover drug agents began to play fast and loose with their own money; undercover organized-crime agents began to have the genuine need of a "family." Looking at it now, Skinny realized that undercover agents weren't the only ones susceptible, though with Nickel it was particularly obvious that that was just what had happened. He had fallen into a role that had overtaken him, and he had lost track of who he was and what he had set out to do—that much was evidenced both by what he had done to Ruth and by what he had not done for Dwayne. As a policeman, you did not beat up one innocent civilian and undermine the search for another, not for the sake of your cover or anything else.

"How long have you been on this?" Skinny asked, putting down the policeman's hat, turning back to Nickel.

"From the beginning?" Nickel asked in reply, then answered his own question, seemingly anxious to say. "Eleven years, on and off."

"Eleven years?" Skinny said, an expression of disbelief

not a question, thinking of the whole, vast time he had been a policeman, how that role had affected him.

"I was in the prison when you were there," Nickel went on. "I saw you once or twice before you left. That was the start. I stayed in the prison for a while, followed up with the people I met. Dropped out for a while, did other things, then went back to it—went back at Ishanti last year when he took over the Lily, found out about the boat."

"Eleven years," Skinny said yet again, distracted, thinking of time. "Has Dryden been running things all along?"

Nickel shook his head no.

"He's new, came into town for one thing, stay on for this other. It's over now, that's why I can tell you. Dryden, he called the end after I was shot."

Skinny did not know what to say to that, so for a moment he said nothing at all. He had the sense he had the information he needed if he could just clear away the clutter and the sick feeling down deep in his gut. He knew he needed time to think.

"Where'd you get that bird?" he asked. "The one you had when I saw you?"

Nickel ventured a smile, sensing that Skinny was getting ready to leave.

"That bird is something," he remarked before he answered. "It's as smart as a child. Evans Charles got it for me."

"I'd like to have one for myself," Skinny said, and pulled open the door, hesitating a moment before leaving, feeling that he had just missed something and trying to figure what, but finally leaving anyway, assuming that it would come to him later.

At the nurses' station he saw the uniformed policeman leaning on the counter, waiting impatiently. He saw the look the policeman gave him, the hard, angry stare; what he did not see was Nickel slumping down in bed, feeling for the tape recorder concealed under his leg, taking it out and verbally marking the end of the tape before he picked up the phone to call his supervisor, William Dryden.

36

William Dryden's office was on the twentieth floor of 1001 Howard, a thirty-story tower building located five blocks from New Orleans's central business district, four blocks from the Poydras Street corridor. Because there were no other tall buildings nearby, the view from the office was unobstructed, and through the windows it was possible to see three bends in the Mississippi River. In the late morning sun, the river was a brilliant, shimmering gold. Tugboats, barges, freighters, tankers, and riverboats of all sizes and types followed the river's broad meandering course.

The office was no smaller than a standard office, about ten feet by twelve feet, but it was made to seem smaller by the amount of furniture and clutter it contained. Around the front of the desk there were three heavy, white-oak chairs of the old-fashioned sort often found in waiting rooms. Beside the desk there were low, wooden bookshelves. On all but one of the chairs, on the desk, on the floor, and on the shelves, there were papers in haphazard stacks, fat file folders held closed by rubber bands, computer printouts, bound and unbound reports.

On the wall over the bookshelves there was a plaque bearing the official seal of the United States Drug Enforcement Administration. The two metal ashtrays on the desk were filled with clumps of half-smoked pipe tobacco and burnt-down kitchen matches.

William Dryden had been told that every day three hundred fifty billion gallons of water passed beneath the twin-span river bridges. That worked out to roughly two hundred forty million gallons a minute, a useless though impressive piece of information he considered as he looked out at the bridges themselves. Coming in through the large, double-paned windows, the sun was warm, very nearly hot on his legs.

Of all the cities he had been assigned to in his thirty-one-year career William Dryden liked New Orleans best. He liked the fact that it was, seemingly, of its own volition removed from the mainstream, remaining, like some isolated outpost in a forever-hostile territory, caught up in its own way of doing things. He liked the food, too, of course—that went without saying—and he liked the vast disparity of the neighborhoods: the French Quarter and the Marigny, the Garden District, Carrollton, Midcity, the Lakefront, the Irish Channel, each one very much like a city unto itself; but what he liked most was that the real city remained hidden behind the clichéd images of it most often presented, the images of jazz funerals and Mardi Gras and high-ceilinged antebellum homes. There was a real city here, all right, very genuine, at most levels even realistic in its outlook, and that made the show better, like discovering that your favorite, apparently eccentric aunt was, beneath her wild costumes and flamboyant makeup, a shrewd, practical, businesslike person, maintaining appearances mainly because those appearances worked to her advantage. The knowledge of the charade forged a bond and gave an increased sense of belonging, of sharing a secret. It brought sly winks and amused smiles when the uninformed were left spellbound by wrought-iron balconies and raised cemeteries and Italianate mansions and tried to order *cush-cush* in French—or, for that matter, when they tried to order *cush-cush* at all. There was a definite sense of place here and a readily available sense of belonging, and while that made it easy to understand why the regional director had suddenly decided to take early retirement and to stay on in New Orleans as a civilian, William Dryden did wish that he had maintained things better before he had left. The office was, literally and figuratively, a mess. Six years before, the special agent had been sent to the New Orleans office to take charge of a single operation. This time, he had been sent to take charge of the whole office until a new director could be appointed. While regional-level duties were being handled in Washington, still his task was, to say the least, daunting. He had charge of all local operations, he had more paperwork than even he could believe, and what was most pressing of all, he had an attitude problem among the agents. Because the former director had been more absent than present, the agents had become accustomed to playing by rules they themselves established, using whatever tactics they chose. The result was an undisciplined, cliquish lot with a suspiciously impressive arrest record, a dangerous circumstance if ever there was one, a situation William Dryden pondered as he tried to comprehend just how much water flowed down that huge river.

Enough to drown you, he said to himself, and turned back to his desk.

The problem with attitude, he felt certain, and the agent's shooting were very much interrelated: one, more than likely, had brought on the other. Which was not to say that there was any justification for it. But if Nickel had gone so far as to beat up a civilian just to maintain his cover, which he had admitted, then there was no telling what other transgressions had been committed. That was why, acting as the director, William Dryden had put a stop to the operation and why he had put in a call to the ATF. He wanted to make it very clear from the outset that he would not tolerate such nonsense. He was serving notice that the slack times were over. He would let the ATF appear to take charge of the case, and he would move on very cautiously, investigating the shooting himself, staring down the sullen, resentful looks he got from the agents. As far as anyone in the office would know, he felt he had done what he could on this case, and because of the circumstances, he viewed the DEA's continued involvement as more of a liability than an asset—a view he intended to convey to the ATF agent due any minute. And although he wondered if he really was just acting to cover his own ass and to protect the office, regardless of culpability, what prevailed in his mind was the need to accomplish two things: to impose some order on his agents and to control the damage that had already been done. It was, he knew, a judgment call that could very easily be questioned.

William Dryden patted the side pocket of his rumpled suit coat, searching for his pipe. Not feeling it, he patted the pocket on the other side, but it was not there either. An annoyed, preoccupied frown crossed his face, and he began to rummage through the stacks of papers on his desk, looking under and on top of them.

"Help you?" a voice offered.

The special agent glanced up, said, "No. I'll find it," then briefly continued his search.

"Don Gatzke," the man said. "ATF."

William Dryden gave up his search, sat back in his chair, and immediately saw his pipe, the stem of it marking his place in a voluminous report, the bowl protruding.

Don Gatzke was standing in the doorway, both hands in the pockets of his pants, a tentative smile on his face. William Dryden saw that he was a large man in his forties, gone a bit soft. He saw that his sport coat was old and wrinkled, of a faded and indeterminate color that so obviously wouldn't show stains he almost asked him right then how long he had been divorced.

"Come in," he said instead. "Pull up a chair, if you can find one."

Gatzke nodded agreeably, sat down in the one available chair, and crossed his legs, exposing a band of white, hairless skin between the top of his short sock and the cuff of his trousers. He made no secret of inspecting the office, his small eyes roving before they came back to William Dryden. Gatzke had heard about this special agent, about how he was scrupulous about regulations and merciless to those who broke them, from looking at him an assessment he had no trouble believing. With his thin shoulders and slight build he looked more like a book-keeper than a field agent; behind his glasses his eyes were bright, clear blue and hard as glass.

"Thanks for coming," William Dryden said.

"Sorry about missing your call yesterday," Gatzke replied, smiling apologetically. "I was out of the office all day."

William Dryden dismissed that with a wave.

"It gave me time to go over your report." He continued the wave to include all the papers stacked in the office. "It's here somewhere. Interesting reading."

Gatzke did not say anything to that but put his elbows

on the arms of the chair and interlaced his fingers, starting to look around again.

"Just out of curiosity," the special agent asked, "how did you get involved?"

"It's all in the report," Gatzke replied. "The coast guard got the call and passed it on to us." He shrugged. "I had the weekend duty."

"That's right," William Dryden said as if chiding himself, focusing. "Is that why you allowed the complainants to keep the boy? Because it was the weekend?"

"Partly," Gatzke admitted, his eyes squinting just a little. "But mainly because our office is closed on Sundays. If I had taken him, I'd have had to put him in the youth home. That's the rule." He paused. "You ever been to the youth home?"

William Dryden shook his head no.

"You ought to go sometime. It's a cross between an orphanage and a prison. It's run by social workers, but there's a nine-foot chain-link fence around the perimeter. Very tough place. I'd hate to be there when they turn out the lights. Some of those kids are bigger than I am. Mean bastards, too, a lot of them. But if I had to do it again, I would. I'd put his ass in there. Fuck him. Give him something to compare to when he moves up to Angola." He smiled pleasantly. "I've had to explain this before."

William Dryden was quick to separate the mixed signals in Gatzke's reply, but he did not immediately know how to read them. There was a crassness about Gatzke he did not really like, but he did not want to judge the man based only on his crude speech or, for that matter, on his beefy face and thick, fleshy neck. He removed his pipe from the report and re-marked his place with a pencil.

"What about the gun?" he went on. "The one mentioned in the supplemental report?"

"It's hard to go by a description."

"Speculation?"

Gatzke shrugged, his reply.

William Dryden thumped the bowl of the pipe against his palm, then dropped the tobacco dislodged into one of the two ashtrays on his desk. He cleared the stem by blowing through it once or twice. He understood now what Gatzke was doing, giving the appearance of cooperation while volunteering nothing, and he decided to try to put him off-balance.

"Well, it's up to you now anyway. As of Monday, I shut down our operation." He took out a bag of tobacco, unfolded the foil top, and began to fill his pipe. He returned the pleasant smile Gatzke had shown him a few moments before and said nothing more. He could see Gatzke thinking that over.

"Your man wasn't shot until Tuesday," Gatzke said finally. "Tuesday night."

"I won't ask how you know that," William Dryden replied easily. "But you're right." With his thumb he pressed down the tobacco. "I let him stay out to try to find the boy—he got himself shot instead."

Gatzke blinked once, the skin around the corners of his eyes crinkling into little puzzled lines, then he blinked again.

"I assume your office is running an operation," William Dryden went on, "and what I want you to know is, as far as this office is concerned, you've got a clear deck."

Gatzke started to say something, but William Dryden held up his hand, palm flat and facing out in a way that indicated he did not want to hear anything about the ATF's operation, not even a denial of its existence.

"You'll get full cooperation on this end, anything we can do."

Don Gatzke was put off-balance, all right, made uncertain what to say. To acknowledge William Dryden's offer of cooperation was to admit that there was, in fact, an operation; and to say nothing was to create a suspicion. He could deny the whole thing, of course, but to lie outright to a regional director, even an acting one, particularly after one of his agents had been shot, was not something readily explained. And there was William Dryden, looking at him with those eyes, waiting. Unaware that he was doing so, Don Gatzke pushed his right fist into his left hand until the middle knuckle popped.

"We'll clean up our own mess," William Dryden went on finally, taking him off the hook. "I served the search warrant on the policeman who shot Anthony Toin myself. We'll nail him down, but that's it for us."

Gatzke looked off, out the window, his uncertainty showing in his expression. He looked back when the phone rang.

William Dryden said, "Excuse me," before he answered it. He listened intently for a moment, then put his hand over the mouthpiece. "I better take this," he said.

Gatzke nodded curtly.

"Let me know if there's any way I can help you," William Dryden added.

Don Gatzke stood up, took one final look at William Dryden, and left, wondering just what that had been all about. In one way he felt he had made a lucky escape, but in another way he felt, rather than escaping, he had been sucked into something he did not really understand. What he couldn't get past were those hard, uncompromising eyes that made him feel naked.

"Thank you," William Dryden said into the phone, and hung it up, pleased that he had told his secretary to buzz him a few minutes after the ATF agent had arrived. He rolled his weight onto one hip and reached into his pants pocket for matches. He lit his pipe then waved his hand over it, with one motion both extinguishing the match and clearing away the smoke. Idly, he looked at the framed picture of his wife and daughter he kept on the corner of his desk.

Eleven years before, after their relationship had deteriorated badly, William Dryden and his wife had been divorced after nineteen years of marriage. In a relatively short period of time, it seemed to him, his wife's personality had changed. She had begun to make unreasonable demands of him and to behave erratically, her moods shifting unpredictably. She had not seemed to know what she wanted to do with her life—except to be very certain the life she had was not the one that she wanted. William Dryden had regarded the changes in her with both sadness and anger, attributing them to a midlife crisis, and when she had demanded a divorce, he had given her one, not knowing what else he *could* do. Three months after the divorce had been finalized, she had been diagnosed with inoperable brain cancer. And although the doctors had tried to assure him that the tumor was not necessarily the cause of the changes in her personality, he had never believed them; his daughter had never really forgiven him for leaving his wife, her mother, when she had needed him most. In trying to put his life back together, in trying to give himself a reason to go on, he had looked for some sense to those events, some underlying order; and although he had never found either, what he had learned was to look for causes that were not readily apparent, the small indications of unseen forces at work.

From his brief meeting with Agent Gatzke, William Dryden had learned two things—at least, all the indications were there. He felt certain the ATF *had* been running an operation, likely connected to the type of gun both described in the supplemental report and used to shoot Agent Toin. And he had learned that despite the evidence to the contrary, the motive and the weapon, he was not at all certain the New Orleans detective had shot his agent. There were too many things that didn't add up, indications of forces *not* there. Why, for example, would the detective have mentioned the gun on the boat if he had kept it? And why would he use *that* gun? And why would he announce his intentions? There were other nagging inconsistencies, too, elements of motive and sequence he had just begun to explore when his direct-line phone rang again.

"This is Nickel," Anthony Toin identified himself.

"Go ahead," William Dryden replied, still mulling over his interview with Gatzke.

"The man just here," Nickel went on, his voice flat and restrained in a way that revealed his anxiety. "Just left. The skinny New Orleans cop might'a shot me."

"Shot you when?" William Dryden asked, somewhat surprised by his own question, realizing how his mind was still on the inconsistencies apparent. "Shot you Tuesday night or shot you this morning?"

"Either one," Nickel replied very dryly. "The man did it. Got it on tape. Say, 'Why didn't you call me?' like, if he'd of known, wouldn't have done it."

William Dryden thought that over for a moment but could reach no conclusion.

"Did he try to convince you he didn't do it?"

"No," Nickel replied. "Just asked questions, like he trying to figure a way out."

Or trying to figure out who did it, William Dryden said to himself. "I'll send someone over to pick up the tape," he said to Anthony Toin.

37

Although she had been in the hospital only a relatively short time, to Ruth it had been entirely too long. There was an air of unreality in the hospital, a sense of being on hold. And while she knew it was in some instances better to err on the side of caution, toward the end of her stay she had the feeling that caution and the quality of her insurance were playing about equal roles—a feeling reinforced when she reviewed the bill. For the tablet of aspirin she had been given that morning she had been charged twelve dollars.

"So the way I see it," she had remarked, "I'll send you a bottle of five hundred aspirin and we'll call it just about even."

"Your insurance will cover everything but the first two hundred fifty dollars," the billing clerk had replied, as if that made it okay to charge whatever they wanted.

Ruth had been fit to be tied. What bothered her most, finally, was that rather than feeling grateful for the services rendered, as she left the hospital she felt she had been scammed. She resolved to do something about it, but as soon as she went outside, her anger diminished.

The sunlight seemed vastly more important than an in-flated bill, which she knew was an entirely normal response. Still, as she waited on the curb for a cab, she couldn't help noticing all the extravagantly expensive cars in the doctors' parking lot across the street and calculating all the twelve-dollar aspirin dispensed to buy and maintain them.

Being confined, Ruth realized, had heightened her perceptions. The sky seemed exceptionally blue. The air seemed to carry with it a particular quality, a thinness, like the fall light. The smell of the cab was both pungent and musty.

"You from out of town?" the cab driver asked her.

"No," Ruth replied, assuming that that was his standard opening question.

"Most people, they get a nose job, they go out of town."

"Yes, I guess they do," Ruth replied, though she did not offer anything further.

Thereafter the ride passed without conversation, a series of images very appropriate to New Orleans: a section of sidewalk lifted and broken by the roots of a huge oak tree, an iron fence settling in places, the sections forming long, low angles, a view down St. Charles of a streetcar.

When the cabbie turned onto her street, Ruth noticed right away the Cadillac parked in front of her house; and when she saw the size of the man sitting inside it, her first reaction was fear, then outraged anger.

"Can you call the police on your radio?" she asked the cabbie.

"Sure can," he replied.

"Then call them," she ordered, "and wait until they

get here." And with that she threw open the door of the cab even before it stopped rolling. "That's the man who gave me my nose job," she said hotly, one foot on the pavement.

Ruth saw the door of the Cadillac open and the man get out. She saw that it wasn't the man who had beaten her—this man was, if anything, even bigger. Then she saw the door on the other side of the car open, too, and she saw Dwayne get out. She half-ran to that side of the car and bent down beside him, putting her hands on his shoulders, feeling up and down his arms as if feeling for broken bones. She kept one hand on him and stood up, turning to the enormous black man, her eyes angry and accusing, demanding an explanation.

"The boy wanted to see you," Ishanti lied. "Brought him by."

Ruth again turned her attention to Dwayne, this time noticing his brand-new blue jeans, stiff as cardboard, his new high-topped white sneakers and multicolored T-shirt.

"It looks like you've been shopping," she said, smiling briefly.

" 'Shanti took me this morning," Dwayne said. "Went to the store."

From the way that he said it Ruth knew that Dwayne's trip to the store had been a first for him, an adventure; she felt an astonishment, then a sadness.

"Well, you look great," she made sure to say.

Ruth glanced at Ishanti, still uncertain of him, trying to remember what Skinny had told her, saw the cab off to her left, the driver anxiously waiting, and in that moment made her decision.

"I've got coffee inside," she said to Ishanti. "And cookies," she said to Dwayne.

"Here to talk to you," Ishanti replied, apparently accepting the invitation. "Want to hear what happened to your face."

After Ruth had paid the cab driver and instructed him to cancel the call to the police, the three of them had gone on into her apartment, Ruth first, then Dwayne, then Ishanti. Ruth had picked up the three days' mail from the floor and put it on the table in the front hall. She had put her purse down in the same place, wondered whether or not she should leave it there, then felt guilty for even thinking it. Her apartment seemed both too small and too big—too big for Dwayne, too small for Ishanti—a situation she resolved by showing Ishanti into the living room and taking Dwayne with her into the kitchen. Dwayne sat at the small table, the cookie jar open and within easy reach, as Ruth made coffee, feeling surprisingly awkward but very relieved. The small chore completed, Ruth sat at the table with Dwayne.

"So where have you been?" she asked. She took a cookie for herself. "What have you been doing?" She started to take a bite of the cookie, felt a sharp twinge in her jaw, and just held it. "Other than shopping?" she added with a half smile.

Dwayne shrugged.

"Nothing," he said, then, "What happened to your face?"

It took an effort for Ruth not to touch the bandage across her nose.

"I was coming to see you," she replied, sitting up a little straighter, her voice earnest and soft. "Like I had promised."

Ishanti came in from the living room and stood in the

doorway, seeming to fill it completely. After a moment he leaned against one side of the door frame, both hands in his pockets.

"I had just left my office," Ruth continued, speaking to Dwayne but for Ishanti, her tone now underlaid with the insult she felt. "Two men forced me into an alley. They wanted to know where *you* were, but I wouldn't tell them. One of them got very angry." Her eyes locked on Ishanti's eyes. "He beat me."

"What he look like?" Ishanti asked, his tone hard and matter-of-fact, without regret or apology.

"He was big," Ruth replied. "Almost as big as you are."

"I remembered where your house was," Dwayne interjected with obvious pride.

"Man who beat you," Ishanti said, "he called Nickel. Got a temper."

"Got shot," Dwayne observed. "I seen it."

"You saw him get shot?"

Dwayne nodded, an acknowledgment that took Ishanti by surprise, too.

"He seen your boyfriend drive by," Ishanti explained, "just before it happened."

Dwayne nodded again.

"My God," Ruth said softly, immediately thinking she knew what that meant—that Skinny *had* shot Nickel—and feeling the force of her thought.

"Don't think he did it," Ishanti went on. "Don't think he that stupid." He pushed himself to a standing position by flexing his shoulder, and the top of his head very nearly touched the underside of the door frame. "Know something missing. Come to see you, hope I see what." For a moment his eyes were thoughtful. "Been in the prison," he added, an observation about Skinny Ruth mistook as an attempt to explain his concern.

She heard the coffee finish dripping, got up from the table, went to the cupboard, and got out two mugs. When she turned back, she saw that Ishanti had moved to her chair. In a low voice he said something to Dwayne.

Dwayne took another cookie from the cookie jar, hesitated, reached back and took another. Without looking at Ruth, he got up and left the kitchen.

The front door opened and closed.

"Told him to wait outside," Ishanti explained.

Ruth crossed her arms and leaned back against the counter. Ishanti did not seem inclined to say anything, so she didn't either; and after a while, after her initial apprehension had passed, she realized she did not know what *to* say. She wanted to believe that Skinny was innocent. She knew she wanted what was best for Dwayne. But her intentions and what she should *do* seemed separated by a vast gulf of not knowing—though about Dwayne she questioned whether she did, in fact, know and was just giving herself a way out by pretending not to.

"I take a cup of that coffee," Ishanti reminded her. "Take it black."

Ruth turned back to the counter, filled both mugs, took them and put them on the table. She sat across from Ishanti, in the corner, in the chair Dwayne had left. For a moment she studied Ishanti, noting his broad, sloping brow and broad nose, trying to read his dark, sloe eyes. For some reason what came to mind was the night Dwayne's aunt had been killed, later on, driving past the housing project with Skinny, when she had first considered all the orbits and connections in that small city, when she had first gotten the sense of a world she had often passed by but had never stopped to consider.

"What's it like?" she wanted to ask, but she knew that she couldn't.

"What do you do for a living?" she asked instead, and immediately felt awkward for asking it.

"Run nightclubs," Ishanti replied. "Keep 'em solid."

Ruth did not know what he meant by that, and her question showed in her expression.

Ishanti sat forward tentatively, careful not to lean too much and to put too much weight on the small table. The coffee mug was lost from view between his huge hands.

"Where I live, ain't got no country club. Ain't got no golf course." He uncovered the mug and took a sip of coffee, his observation gaining strength from his matter-of-factness, the flat tone in his voice. "People still got to make a livin', still got to make deals. Need a place to go where they safe, where they sure nobody hear 'em, be by themselves. That what I do. Tend the bar myself if they want, be there or not. Be solid."

Ruth considered that, knowing better than to ask what kind of deals.

"Don't allow no drugs," Ishanti added, reading her very first thought. "Don't want nothing to do with 'em."

"Does that man work for you?" Ruth asked. "Nickel? The one who did this?" She waved her hand at her face.

"Used to," Ishanti replied. "Dwayne's father, too—can't exactly put them together." He paused for a moment, and a questioning light came into his eyes, a question he quickly related to himself. "Look like I in the middle. Don't know shit."

"You must know more than you realize."

"I think on it," Ishanti agreed, and he seemed to, though when he spoke again, it was off in a different direction. "Know your boyfriend pulled the boy out the river. Know the two of you brought him back to his auntee."

Ishanti paused and looked down at the coffee mug that seemed so small next to his hands; and in that long moment Ruth felt a flush of excitement and trepidation. She felt certain she knew what he was about to say. The decision was about to be made for her, reinforcement from within Dwayne's own community: he was about to ask her if she would look after Dwayne, and she would say yes, she had counted on it.

"Boy don't have no family," Ishanti went on. "They all gone now, one way or another." He pushed the cookie jar off to one side.

"You don't have to—" Ruth began.

"I going to keep him," Ishanti said. "Take care of him myself, give him a place. Glad you did what you did, saved his life."

Ruth felt her face freeze into a rigid mask; only her eyes seemed able to move. Her blood ran cold, then hot. She was bewildered, uncertain how she could have been so wrong, and immediately she felt a loss.

"My place is too big for just me." Ishanti went on. "Won't be no trouble." He shrugged, heaving his massive shoulders up and down. "Got to find out first who shot Nickel for sure, who blew up the boat—find out if they after the boy."

Ruth just nodded because she did not trust her voice.

"Want to talk to your boyfriend again."

The initial shock passed, and she was thinking again, though it seemed she was just mouthing words.

"I didn't know you had spoken to him at all."

"Yesterday," Ishanti affirmed. "You tell him, tell him I call." He took a final taste of the coffee. "I be in touch with you, too." And with that he stood up, took the coffee mug, and put it into the sink. Before he left, he stopped and looked down at Ruth, but she did not have the energy right then to do more than to glance in his direction.

Ruth heard his footsteps, then she heard the front door open and close. After that, she heard how quiet it was in her apartment, the silence she had often treasured before now seeming an empty, vacuous presence. She had so many thoughts so quickly, back and forth, that it was hard to tell exactly what she was feeling. There was some sadness, she knew, some sense of loss—if she was honest, some relief. But when she realized that she had not said good-bye to Dwayne, she put all that aside and hurried out to catch him, hoping that she was not too late, puzzled when she saw Ishanti coming back up the sidewalk, back toward her door.

"The boy gone," Ishanti said when he saw her, his voice angry. "Not around anywhere. Somebody must'a took him while we were talkin'."

"Dear God," Ruth said in reply, feeling it all starting up again.

38

Skinny had been meaning to get a new gun, and several things prompted him to go gun shopping that afternoon. First, since he was again on suspension, he happened to have a little extra time; and second, in Nickel's hospital room he had noticed the uniformed policeman's 9mm Beretta. It wasn't that he wanted to stop carrying his silver revolver—it made his heart heavy, in fact, to think of it sitting under his bed by itself—it was that, practically speaking, with the advances in design and technology, a revolver just wasn't enough anymore. The new pistols, he had heard, were exceptionally reliable, had a higher rate of fire for the average shooter, and to Skinny's way of thinking what was most important of all, carried a whole lot more bullets, numbers up in the teens. And besides that, he deserved it. He deserved a new gun and a little time to think to go along with it. By any estimation, it had been a very tough week.

So after he had left Nickel's hospital room and after he had called ahead for an appointment, he had driven out Poydras and gotten on the expressway, passing Charity

Hospital and Central Lock-up in the process. He had crossed the causeway, and on the north shore of Lake Pontchartrain kept going north until the low hills and horse country both began at the same time.

Although the hills were soft and rolling and only reached an elevation of a hundred or so feet, to Skinny it was a whole new topography. He felt as if he had wandered off into another state. Past Covington he veered to the right and soon was in an area where the roads were designated by numbers rather than by names. Long stretches of fence fronted the highway. Even though Skinny was never more at home than he was on his boat—usually from New Orleans he went south, toward the Gulf of Mexico, rather than north— still he could readily understand why people lived in this country. The houses were most often set on hill-tops, off by themselves, overlooking swells of land much like a friendly, rolling, grass-covered sea.

Back Pasture and Back Alley Guns was a discovery Skinny had made more or less by accident. He and Theriot had been in the area, interviewing a witness, had seen the sign and stopped in, in time to see a man they later learned was the owner summarily remove five bowl-ing pins from a four-by-eight table with five quick shots from a Springfield .45. Skinny had liked that, liked seeing the owner of a gun shop actually shoot rather than just talk about it, and when the owner had looked at him and said, "Your turn," without any introduction whatsoever, he had liked that, too—until he had discovered that the bowling-pin trick was not quite as easy as it seemed. With his silver gun he had knocked down the pins, all right, but four of the five had stayed on the table. But the owner had stayed right with him, going into his shop and coming back out with a box of heavier bullets and a lightweight video camera. He had made him shoot again and had videotaped him as he did, then had taken him into the shop and made him look at what he had done right and wrong. They had spent several hours like that, back and forth, until the pins had started flying satisfactorily. And while Mike Theriot had thought the man more than a little eccentric—a hard point to argue since, after all, there he had been, all by himself, out in the middle of nowhere, it seemed, making a science of shooting bowling pins off a table—Skinny had liked him just fine. He had liked seeing someone doing something they obviously enjoyed and were good at, no matter how weird, and what was more important to him at the moment, he knew the man's knowledge of guns was encyclopedic.

Near Barker's Corner he veered off again, then turned down a dirt road, and there was the owner, Hamilton Jethro, just where he had left him four months before, twenty-five feet from a four-by-eight table, pistol in hand.

Hamilton was built like an oversize fireplug, with a torso so thick and long it made his arms and legs seem short and stubby. His complexion was a healthy red-tan. He was clean-shaven and had fairly short hair and a reticent good humor that somehow put Skinny in mind of an elf—but, from his build, an elf crossed with a pit bull, an interesting match to consider. When he fired, smoke puffed out of his pistol, directed upward through a Caspian compensator, in one steady stream.

The pins seemed to launch from the table.

He turned to Skinny and said, "What you *need* is a good forty-five," starting up as if their conversation had been uninterrupted. "What you probably *want* is a forty."

"What I want," Skinny noted, "is a lot of big bullets, all in one gun."

Hamilton waved for him to follow and led the way into his shop. On the glass counter was an unopened blue box.

"The major advantage of the forty is dimensional," Hamilton went on. "It's a compromise between the nine millimeter and the forty-five." He slid the box toward Skinny. "The forty holds more bullets than a forty-five, and they're considerably harder-hitting bullets than the nine—increased bullet weight and cross-sectional density give it better terminal ballistics."

"Terminal ballistics," Skinny repeated, smiling brightly. "I like it."

"That's not what that means," Hamilton grumbled, and gestured in a way that indicated that Skinny should open the box.

Inside the dark blue box was a pistol that looked rather like a shortened Colt government model that had been partially melted. There were no sharp edges on it at all. While both the low-profile sights and the wraparound grip were flat black, the rest of the pistol was a matt stainless steel.

"A silver gun," Skinny said with evident pleasure. He immediately picked it up and pointed it, waving it in short arcs, admiring its muzzle-heavy balance. "How many bullets does it hold?"

"Eleven in the magazine and one in the chamber," Hamilton replied.

Skinny's head jerked around.

"Twelve bullets in this little gun?"

Hamilton nodded.

"Now *that's* Skinny," Skinny observed, holding the gun up close to his face to inspect it again. "Let's shoot something."

By way of reply, Hamilton reached to the floor, then set a bowling pin up on the counter.

After they had been at it two hours, after they had done terminal damage to quite a number of pins, between rounds Skinny asked Hamilton, "Have you ever seen a pistol with a select fire capability that's a little bigger than a Colt automatic?"

Hamilton was inspecting the last set of pins they had shot, but he stopped.

"The receiver housing is glass reinforced," Skinny went on, "some kind of plastic. It's gas-operated, locked-breech, small caliber but high velocity, probably a centerfire."

"About this long?" Hamilton asked, holding his hands apart a little over a foot.

Skinny nodded.

Apparently satisfied that the pin he was inspecting was in passable shape, Hamilton set it up on the table.

"It's called a Scamp," he said as he walked back toward the bench at the twenty-five-foot line. "I've never seen one, but I have seen pictures."

"Do you know anything about it?"

Hamilton picked up a magazine from the bench and began to mash flat-pointed bullets down into it.

"A little," he replied. He loaded another magazine before he went on, apparently organizing his thoughts as he slid in the bullets. "During World War Two and Korea, our main battle rifle was the M-1 Garand, which was heavy. Depending on the piece of wood used for the stock, it could weigh up to eleven pounds. And we had

forty-fives. The forty-five pistol was, as much as anything, a badge of rank for the officers. They were never
really intended to use it to defend themselves, not in a
battlefield situation. But the officers and others like
radio men, who had a lot to carry, didn't particularly
want an eleven-pound rifle in addition to everything
else."

Hamilton put the two loaded magazines down on the
bench next to Skinny's new gun.

"A man who was in prison at the time came up with
the idea to make a lighter rifle to bridge the gap between
the forty-five and the M-1 Garand. The rifle would be
heavier than the forty-five, but it would have considerably
more power and firepower—and it would be considerably
lighter than the Garand. The rifle was eventually accepted
and produced as the M-1 Carbine."

Hamilton picked up one of the magazines he had
loaded and inserted it into the pistol.

"The M-1 Carbine," he went on, "sort of fell by the
wayside because the cartridge it fired was pretty much
worthless. It just didn't have enough power, especially
with the full-metal jacket the military has to use to comply
with the Geneva Convention."

He released the slide on the .40, aimed carefully at a
paper target, fired, and missed the black bull's-eye completely, a curious sequence Skinny had observed at least
three times before.

"When our military adopted the M-16 as our main battle rifle," Hamilton continued, unconcerned by his miss,
turning back to Skinny but keeping the pistol pointed
downrange, "someone at Colt had the brilliant idea to
make an M-16 into a rifle-pistol, an even smaller version
of the M-1 Carbine. All they forgot was, it didn't make

sense to have a different rifle anymore, since the M-16 is so light—it only weighs about five pounds."

"And the rifle-pistol they made was the Scamp?"

"Right," Hamilton affirmed. "A great idea about forty years too late. The military wouldn't buy it. There was no commercial market because it fired full-automatic. To my knowledge, there was only one manufacturing run."

When Skinny took a moment to consider that, recalling the brief look he had had at the Scamp, Hamilton turned into the pistol he held pointed downrange and took down five pins with five shots.

"Why do you miss the target," Skinny asked, "then hit the pins?"

Hamilton shrugged as he cleared the pistol, ejecting both the magazine and the round in the chamber before he decocked the hammer.

"I flinch," he admitted, "but when I shoot fast, I flinch opposite the recoil, *into* the target."

Skinny considered that, too, remembering the way the muzzle had jerked when Hamilton had pulled the trigger on a misfeed that hadn't gone off.

"I have gun magazines that go back for years," Hamilton added. "If you have the time, I can find you a picture of the Scamp."

Skinny nodded, accepting that offer and accepting the fact that Hamilton was picking up, getting ready to go on inside; and as he bent down to retrieve the spent brass, it occurred to him that, as good as he was with a pistol, Hamilton would be even better if he took the time to go back to bull's-eye. Although Hamilton could clear the table more quickly than he could, still Skinny had had enough formal instruction to know that you had to learn to hit what you aimed at before you accelerated the process. There was a logical sequence to learning, certain steps to be taken, and the fundamentals had to come first—an observation that he immediately related to his present predicament.

He saw an empty casing beneath the bench and moved that way to pick it up.

He had quite literally plunged right into the middle of a situation, and was now suffering its consequence, without having taken the time to study the basics, without having spent time on the sequence. He felt certain he had all the information he needed if he could just sort it out.

He retrieved the casing beneath the bench just as Hamilton picked up the can of unfired ammunition. Weighted down heavily with two pistols, a tool box, the can of ammunition, and the PACT timer, Hamilton paused only a moment before he trudged off.

"You get the brass," he suggested, "and I'll start looking through magazines."

"Good," Skinny replied, glad to have a few minutes to himself.

Most of the brass had dropped into a fairly small circular area, but a few rounds had scattered. Skinny stayed pretty much in one place, stepping away only when he saw a round that had fallen long or short.

After the boat had exploded, after he had pulled Dwayne out of the river, Ruth and he had taken Dwayne to Ruth's apartment. Along the way, he had called the coast guard, and after that he had called the Silver Lily, trying to reach Dwayne's auntee. If the shooter *had* been after the boy, for whatever reason, he had to have known first of all that the boy had survived the explosion; and he had to have known pretty much when Ruth and he were taking him home to Agnes because he was already there waiting.

"So who knew?" he asked himself. "Who *could* have known?"

On the ground the brass kicked out by Hamilton's .45 was not distinguishable from the brass kicked out by the .40. He had to look at each piece before he tossed it into one of the two boxes Hamilton had left on the bench.

He had spoken with Henry the bartender and told him, of course, but he couldn't believe it was Henry. It was too easy to picture Henry and Agnes together. He could too readily feel Henry's loss. And while Henry might have told Nickel, that didn't fit either, since Nickel himself had been shot—and besides that, even Nickel wouldn't go *that* far to maintain his cover.

A peculiar piece of brass caught Skinny's attention, a bigger piece that didn't belong. He picked up the hull of a .44 magnum and folded it into his palm.

It could have been Ishanti, he knew. Ishanti could have blown up the boat. He could have been watching from one bank of the river or the other and seen that Dwayne got away. And Henry could have told *him* when to expect Dwayne. But if that were the case, why had he shot Nickel? Why had he removed the logical suspect and put himself in his place?

Skinny finished picking up the brass in the circular area and started looking for stray random pieces.

Evans Charles, Agnes Charles, Nickel. Evans was killed for business reasons. Agnes was next because she got in the way: Dwayne was the target. Then why Nickel? Nickel could have blown his cover, but that didn't seem likely—from what Skinny had seen, he had worked pretty hard to maintain it.

Partially hidden by the leg of the bench, Skinny saw three tarnished casings that had fallen together. When he retrieved them, he saw that they were three different calibers.

And what about the gun? he asked himself. *The Scamp? And what about that big bird?*

He picked up the three casings and compared them to the .44 still in his hand. He arranged them by caliber, smallest to largest—9mm, .40, .44, .45—idly noting that the caliber did not necessarily determine the length of the brass.

Guns out, drugs in, he said to himself, *but no one has ever found any drugs.*

He stood the four pieces of brass on the bench. In the sequence one caliber was missing.

So who knew? he asked himself again. *Who could have known?*

From somewhere nearby a great blue heron took flight, flapping its enormous wings with air-popping snaps. It flew directly over the shooting range, near the bowling-pin table, and when its shadow passed over the ground, it was as big as the shadow cast by a low-flying airplane.

"I wonder if he has to have a license to fly that thing," Skinny said aloud, then quickly looked at the casings he had left on the bench. For a long moment he stood trans-fixed because he knew, and he knew that he knew before he knew why.

"He *would* have to," he said aloud, not, of course, meaning the heron. "It *would* require a license."

And wherever there was legal regulation there were those who worked around it. Nickel had gotten his bird from Evans Charles, a bird that Ruth had told him was very expensive. Where there was one there were bound to be more. Evans's boat could have held a whole flock of birds in the space made available when the guns were off-loaded.

The guns.

In the sequence of casings he had set on the bench one

caliber was missing: the standard police .38. He hadn't noticed the gap in the sequence because he was so accustomed to seeing it. His revolver was so much a part of him—it was so much a part of his personal scenery—that the brass it produced had been all but invisible, as easily overlooked as a policeman doing his job.

Skinny felt a surge of excitement and at the same time he tasted disgust. He picked up the four casings and held them in one hand, shaking them, making them rattle.

Hamilton came back outside carrying a magazine and called to Skinny.

"Found it," he said.

"I found it, too," Skinny replied, his voice too low to be heard, "but I wouldn't call that bastard a scamp."

39

Mike Theriot felt he was reasonably accustomed to Skinny. He felt he knew Skinny well enough not to be thrown by his unpredictability—he took an odd sort of pride, in fact, in remaining unflappable, giving the appearance, at least, of not being perturbed by whatever he did. But when Skinny called up, talking about birds and select fire guns and telling him to check out a federal agent, Mike Theriot knew he had flapped. He had heard the incredulity and protest in his own voice, and if Skinny had not been so adamant he was sure this time he would *not* have done what he asked. Nevertheless, he had called the ATF office and asked for Don Gatzke and had been told that he was out in the field. Just in case that was a line he had gone by the office and gone through the parking garages nearby looking for a dark blue unmarked police car with oversize tires. From his car he had called the DEA office and spoken to the agent in charge, and after that he had gone by to see Ruth, glad to learn that she had been sent home from the hospital, glad, finally, to be doing something that made sense, both pleased and displeased when he saw a dark blue unmarked police car parked at the curb, not fifty feet from her house. On the corner there was a small neighborhood restaurant. There were two trucks making deliveries and the cars of a few customers early for lunch. Taking advantage of that vehicular activity, very quickly for him, he parked behind a large van and waited, hoping that Skinny would soon get back within radio range, agitated more than a little when he saw a white man he presumed to be a federal agent pick up a black boy from in front of Ruth's house and carry him under his arm to the car.

After William Dryden had listened to the tape of the conversation between Nickel and Skinny, he had rewound it and listened again, absently puffing his pipe, listening the second time more to nuances and inflections of speech than for what he had missed. The conversation affirmed for him the suspicion he already had, that the New Orleans detective was not so much trying to figure a way out for himself as he was trying to figure out who had shot Nickel—though for the life of him he could not say precisely why. There was a genuineness to the detective's tone, he supposed, a very real outrage and anguish, and the range of his questions were more indicative of a search than of something concealed. In one way he agreed with him, too: Nickel should have called him and told him what had happened. But to do that Nickel would have had to admit his mistake, something even now Nickel was not prone to do. And although William Dryden did not know what the detective had meant when he had referred to the bird, he had a feeling he was about to find out, since the detective's partner had called him and asked him to stand by.

William Dryden swiveled his chair around, picked up the binoculars he kept on the floor, looked out the window. Far upriver he saw a shack built out on a pier over the water. For a moment he studied it, the image shimmering in the thick, optic air, then he dropped the binoculars down to chin level. When he looked again, he saw another similar shack, and then another, at the same time his private-line telephone began to ring.

Don Gatzke knew he had more than enough justification to pick up the boy—the boy had, of course, been reported missing and he was, potentially, the sole witness to a murder. So while the ATF agent knew he could be as brazen as he cared to be, still he approached the prospect with some caution, if only because he did not want to tangle with the gorilla-sized monkey who seemed to have appointed himself the boy's protector. When he saw Dwayne come out of Ruth's house by himself and sit down on the front steps, Don Gatzke decided to give it a couple of minutes to see whether or not Ishanti would come out right behind him. He drummed his fingers on the wheel of the car, whistled tunelessly, checked his wristwatch twice in ten seconds. Once, he pulled at the short sleeve of his shirt, pulling it away from his armpit, dropped his nose into the material, and sniffed, assessing his smell, judging it to be about what it should be, all things considered. Not that it bothered him, but since the day before he had pretty much been in his car, first following Skinny, then after Skinny had met with Ishanti outside the prison, following him, figuring he was more likely to come up with the boy—which he had.

Obviously bored, Dwayne got up from the steps and began to wander away from the house.

From the prison, Gatzke had followed Ishanti to the west bank, but when Ishanti had just gone home and parked, after a while Gatzke had decided to pass by the Silver Lily to see if the boy showed up there. He hadn't seen Dwayne, but he had seen Skinny; and not long after that he had seen Nickel, which was when everything had clicked into place. He knew Skinny was after Nickel for beating up Ruth, and he knew Nickel was a DEA agent— Skinny had told him. So if Nickel was shot and Skinny was blamed for the shooting—he was, after all, the logical suspect—except for the small matter of the boy, Gatzke knew he was in the clear. With both the DEA and the local police out of the picture, *he* was the sole agent in place, the only one who could possibly piece together what had happened. Of course William Dryden had withdrawn the DEA from the case: he didn't have much choice.

Don Gatzke started to stretch out but stopped.

"Come to papa," he whispered hopefully, willing Dwayne to come out as far as the sidewalk. "Come to papa."

Dwayne stopped to examine the leaves on the low branches of the fig tree in the front yard before he continued, looking down, admiring his brand-new white sneakers.

Nickel had taken his time about getting out of his car. He had patted his hair, adjusted his collar to look very casual, rotated the gold chain he wore around his neck. By the time he was satisfied with his appearance, Gatzke had gotten the Scamp out of the trunk and moved within firing range. It had surprised him considerably when someone else had opened up on Nickel, too, not that that mattered either. For all he knew it *had* been Skinny, which was even a nice sort of touch. What did matter was that later on, he picked up Ishanti again and saw that he had found the boy; and since then Gatzke had been waiting for him to give him an opportunity to snatch him.

When Dwayne neared the sidewalk, he bent down to wipe a speck of dirt from the top of his shoe.

Going to see Ruth and explaining to her why Skinny was the number-one suspect, that had been pure inspiration. And she had soaked it up, he had seen that, the seed already germinated there in her mind, just like his own wife, always willing to believe the worst possible things about him.

My ex-*wife*, he reminded himself.

Dwayne reached the sidewalk and turned to his right, away from the unmarked blue car.

For a large man, Don Gatzke moved surprisingly quickly. He threw open the door of the car and got out, all in one motion. He crossed the street at a half run. Dwayne had hardly glanced up from his shoes when Gatzke had him, up and under one arm. He carried him across the street, back to his car, and shoved him in ahead of himself through the door he had left open. He started the car and pulled away from the curb, checking his watch, whistling again, stopping when he saw that Dwayne was watching him.

"So how's life in little-monkey land?" he asked, smiling a pained smile but obviously pleased with himself.

40

Skinny drove back across Lake Pontchartrain as fast as his truck allowed. An out-of-balance front tire kept him on the verge of driver control, which was always a factor anyway, even at much slower speeds. Somewhere near the middle of the huge lake his radio came within working range, and he was finally able to get a call through. Over the noise made by the wind, the hopping front tire, and the limit-of-range radio static, he said to William Dryden, "He's been getting it from *me*," speaking about Don Gatzke so loudly William Dryden had to hold his telephone away from his ear. "He's been asking, and I've been telling him. *That's* where he's been getting his information. I thought he was just being lazy about his investigation, always wanting to know what I had learned, but he was pumping me."

The static cleared suddenly, a lack of interference Skinny did not really notice.

"You check out those guns," he went on. "They're called Scamps. Somewhere along the line they were in ATF custody. I'd bet on it. He stole them, and Evans

Charles was selling them for him. That's why he blew up the boat: he was trying to eliminate witnesses."

Skinny listened for a reply, but there was none—or, at least, none that he could hear.

"Maybe Agnes Charles knew that or maybe she just got between him and the boy. But he's after the boy now, that's for sure."

Up ahead, a marked police car was going at much slower speed. Skinny took his police parking permit from under the seat and held it flat against the rear window of the truck.

"What about Anthony Toin?" William Dryden asked.

"He shot your agent to get you off his back," Skinny replied, finding it a little difficult to do three things at once. "He knew you'd drop everything else to find the shooter. And I looked so good for it. I told him I was after Nickel and he probably figured the same thing you did about the gun."

Skinny passed the police car on the right, wiggling the placard up and down.

"But your people never should have been working the case in the first place," he continued, "because there never were any drugs."

The police car jumped ahead and got right on the truck's tail. Skinny dropped the parking permit and showed the blue police light he sometimes left on the dash. The police car responded by turning on the flashing red lights in the light bar.

Skinny pulled over to the right.

The police car passed and began to lead the way.

"My guess is," he added, "Evans Charles was bringing in exotic birds—ask your man where he got his."

William Dryden did not say anything to that because

he already knew where Nickel had gotten his bird. He had heard Skinny ask.

At the end of the bridge Skinny waved his thanks to the police car, and the policeman inside it waved back. Suddenly, a beep tone sounded and a second voice came on the line, a bored-sounding operator advising Skinny that he had a 108-call, a policeman needing assistance. Reflexly—and without another word to William Dryden— he broke the connection and waited as the call was patched through, not surprised to hear from Mike Theriot but surprised to hear the high level of anxiety in his voice.

"He has the boy in the car with him," Mike Theriot began excitedly, the words rushing out. "They're headed downtown. I saw him grab him, right in front of Ruth's house."

"In front of Ruth's house?" Skinny said, then realized he had asked the wrong question first. "*Who* has him?"

"The ATF agent. Big guy, right? Short curly hair? Short sleeves and a tie?"

Skinny refrained from pointing out that he didn't know exactly what Gatzke was *wearing*.

"Where are you?" he asked instead.

Mike Theriot did not reply for a moment and Skinny knew he was only then noting where he was.

"We're on Prytania, coming up on Jackson. I'm two cars back."

Skinny made the turn onto the ramp that led to the expressway. With the sudden change in direction, the truck's tires squealed and the rear end started to come around.

"Stay with him, Theriot," Skinny ordered, fighting the wheel, backing off the gas just a little, seeing that the needle on the truck's temperature gauge was indicating red. "And stay with me. Keep this line open."

Theriot clicked his mike twice in reply.

Skinny tried not to think as he wove in and out of the early afternoon traffic, hearing the truck's engine begin to knock. He tried not to think about the boy, and he tried not to think about whether he could prove enough to make a case against Gatzke—whether William Dryden could make a better case against *him*. As he went over the eight-lane overpass, feeling a heaviness and a surge at the start of the incline, he tried not to think about Ruth, about how Dwayne happened to be in front of her house and why she hadn't called.

"You still with me?" he asked Mike Theriot.

"Coming up on Poydras," Theriot replied. "He's taking a right, toward the river."

"I'm ten minutes away," Skinny guessed.

Past the overpass the expressway leveled out before it started up again, and Skinny was right at that juncture, on a low hump, when he felt the truck's engine lose power, not sputtering at all, just fading. The needle on the temperature gauge indicated an area past red. Skinny took the next exit, Claiborne, his heart sinking as the truck went slower and slower.

"Where are you?" he asked Theriot.

"At the foot of Poydras," Theriot replied, "near the Hilton. Wait."

Skinny smelled the heat coming off the truck's engine In his mind's eye he saw the Hilton and the big blue *H* on top of it, glass elevators moving up and down its side.

"He's in line for the Algiers ferry," Theriot reported, a momentary relief in his voice. "I'm three cars behind him. We're stopped."

"Where's the ferry?" Skinny asked as his truck rolled to a halt. "Where's the ferry?" He could almost hear Theriot looking around.

"It's just leaving the west bank," Theriot replied finally, "just starting this way."

Twenty minutes, Skinny said to himself, surveying the desolate underside of the expressway where he was stranded, knowing that was about how much time he had. *Twenty minutes,* he said again, getting out of the truck, taking the radio with him, quick-stepping down the ramp, arms flapping high.

41

When Ruth moved back inside her apartment, Ishanti went in behind her, not closing the door. For a few moments Ruth and he stood in the hallway, both of them caught up in their own thoughts—Ishanti trying to control his outrage and anger, trying to think reasonably; Ruth dwelling on Dwayne, imagining his fear—then on Ruth's lead they moved into the kitchen.

"Need to find the boy quick," Ishanti said, "or he gone."

Ruth nodded, thinking the very same thing.

"I'll call Skinny," she said, knowing she should have called him a soon as she had seen Dwayne in front of her house.

Ishanti was about to pick up the phone to hand it to her when it rang. He answered it.

Ruth heard him say, "Was about to call you," then she saw him listening intently. "Five minutes," he said, and hung up.

Ruth spotted her keys on the hall table.

"Want us to meet him," Ishanti said. "He downtown.

Say he got the boy under surveillance. Want you to drive."

Ruth did not stop to question that but made for the door, picking up her keys on the way.

Ishanti stepped out behind her.

Ruth locked the door and half-ran to her car. When Ishanti got in, she heard her car sigh and felt it tilt to his side.

Skinny had walked down the exit ramp from the expressway, cut around the Superdome and to Loyola, which was where he met Ishanti and Ruth. Once in the car, he sat in the middle of the backseat, leaning forward, his elbows on his widely spread knees, one foot on either side of the low hump that separated the left floor from the right. After he had given Ruth directions, he told Mike Theriot, "Stand by," then he tapped Ishanti on the shoulder with the radio's antenna.

"Birds, right?" he asked, only partly a question. "Evans Charles was bringing in birds." When Ishanti did not reply right away, he went on, glancing at Ruth in the rearview mirror as he did so. "Evans Charles was taking guns out and bringing exotic birds back. Things went okay until the DEA started working a case against him." Again he tapped Ishanti's shoulder with the radio's antenna. "You know who their man was?" After a moment he answered his own question. "Nickel." He caught Ruth's eye in the mirror. "The guy who beat you up."

"Who has Dwayne?" Ruth asked, her only immediate concern—she could deal with the rest of it later.

"Gatzke," Skinny replied, "which is why we've got a problem."

In the mirror Skinny saw the face Ruth made, her distaste and anger.

"The way I figure it," he went on, "Evans Charles was already running guns when Gatzke flipped to it. He had some guns himself he wanted to sell, so he gave Evans a choice: sell his guns or do time. Okay so far but all those trips out and back made the DEA think there were drugs. With another agency investigating, Gatzke was in a trick. That's why he blew up the boat. When Dwayne survived, Gatzke didn't have any choice but to go after him."

Skinny saw Ruth's expression change from distaste to disgust.

"What's the problem?" Ishanti asked, his eyes fixed straight ahead.

From the way that he said it, Skinny knew that Ishanti didn't see a problem at all: when he found Gatzke he'd just break his back.

"The problem is," Skinny explained, "at this point Gatzke has the right to have Dwayne in custody. Dwayne's wanted two ways, as a runaway and as a witness. Maybe three," he added, checking Ishanti's response. When there was none, he went on. "We've got to be chilly, follow him and see what he's up to."

Ishanti turned his head enough to give Skinny a hard, withering look.

"You one to talk about chilly," he said, obviously referring to the threats Skinny had made when he had last seen him behind the prison.

Skinny raised and dropped both his shoulders at once.

"Yeah, well, I'm sorry about that."

Ruth swung out around a slow-moving tour bus and pulled into the circle in front of the Hilton.

"Hang back," Skinny said as she negotiated the circle. He glanced at the clock in the dashboard, knowing the ferry left punctually on the half hour and the hour. "He's in line for the ferry. Theriot is behind him. We've got a couple of minutes."

Ruth exited the circle three quarters of the way around it and drove the short block to the ferry landing. Both Gatzke and Theriot were hidden from view, on down the ramp.

"We're in line," Skinny said into the radio.

"The gate just opened," Theriot reported. "They're off-loading now."

"I'm coming to you," Skinny replied, and handed his radio to Ishanti. "Press this button to talk," he explained.

Ishanti accepted the radio but did not pay much attention to it.

Skinny opened the door a crack.

"I *am* sorry," he said to Ishanti. "I owe you one."

"I hold you to it," Ishanti replied.

Skinny acknowledged that with a nod.

"Stay in the car," he ordered, "and stay low," and with that he got out and went down the ramp in a crouch. He found Theriot's car and got in.

"Ruth and Ishanti are behind us," he said.

Theriot glanced in the rearview mirror, but before he could say anything the gate opened and the line started forward.

Skinny twisted around so that he was kneeling on the floor, his arms on the seat. He could feel the downward slope of the ramp, then he could feel the gentle sway of the ferry. He heard the heavy drone of the boat's powerful engines.

Theriot took the car out of gear and set the brake.

"Where is he?" Skinny asked.

"On our right front," Theriot replied without looking down.

Skinny adjusted his position, putting more weight on his elbows.

"You did great," he told Mike Theriot, remembering how it had made him feel when Ruth had told him the same thing.

Theriot was sweating profusely.

Skinny knew that the ferry held three cars abreast on a flat deck that encircled the bridge; the upstairs deck was for pedestrians. The trip across the river was free. Once underway, passengers were permitted to get out of their cars, and that was just what he intended to do.

The heavy steel ramp clanged, pulled away, and suddenly the ferry's engines roared to full power. The ferry drifted, caught by the current, before the propellers dug in and very slowly the boat turned, pulling away from the dock, fighting the river every inch of the way.

"He's getting out," Theriot said. "He's got the boy with him."

The engine settled into a less frantic, steadier drone.

"Which way are they going?"

"Up," Theriot replied with a slight jerk of his chin. "Up toward the bow."

"Go around the other way," Skinny ordered, motioning to the far end of the bridge, "but stay back. If they go that way, let them come to you. Tell Ishanti and Ruth to stay in their car."

Skinny popped open the door and got out, bent low, immediately feeling the engines' vibration in the soles of his boots. When he reached Gatzke's car, he stood up a little straighter, enough to look through the car, in time to see Gatzke pull Dwayne around the bridge, out of sight. Gatzke was holding Dwayne's left hand with his right and very obviously holding to it very tightly.

There were few cars on the ferry, and the far side of

the bridge was deserted, a flat expanse of gray steel set off from the broad expanse of the river by a heavy rail made of pipe. By the time he got to the bridge and peered out around it, Gatzke and Dwayne were at the rail, Dwayne struggling somewhat but far overmatched, Gatzke doing something with his free hand, something it took Skinny a long moment to fathom: he was releasing the cable that served as a gate in a three-foot gap in the rail.

Skinny felt his blood run ice-cold because he knew what Gatzke intended to do. It surprised him he hadn't realized it sooner. Dwayne couldn't swim. The river had been known to swallow whole ships. As often as not boats vanished without a trace. In all likelihood a boy Dwayne's size would never be found.

"Hold it right there," Skinny said, but for once his voice wasn't loud enough. It was lost in the roar of the ferry's big diesel engines. "Hold it," he said again, quickly stepping forward, grabbing Dwayne around the waist just as Gatzke got the cable to release. Skinny held Dwayne tightly, and when Gatzke tried to pull him forward, he felt the added resistance. He turned, startled to see Skinny, releasing Dwayne's hand and stepping back toward the now-open gate. He started to smile, his eyes crinkling into the ingratiating uncertainty Skinny remembered from the first time he had met him.

"What are you doing?" he asked.

Skinny picked up Dwayne and held him chest-high, just as he had on the crew boat.

"The big question is," Skinny replied, his anger apparent in his tone, "what are *you* doing?"

Gatzke put both his hands behind his back, leaning forward in the effort, a move that made Skinny realize Dwayne was blocking his access to his new silver gun, a belated consideration made much more serious when Gatzke came out with the Scamp that had been tucked down low in his belt. For a moment he examined the odd-looking rifle-pistol, turning it over and back, then he flung it to the side suddenly, a short toss that landed it in the river.

"Oops," Gatzke said, looking back from the splash, smiling again, this time more genuinely. "Wasn't that the gun you found on the boat?" He put both his hands into his hip pockets, palms flat against his hips. "The case against you is pretty strong, Skinny. All the elements are there: ability, opportunity, motive—especially motive. Your own girlfriend believes you shot Nickel. Without that gun"—he nodded toward the river—"you can't even *dis*prove the rest, much less make a case against me."

Skinny felt his heart sink because he knew that what Gatzke was saying was true. Without the gun, without something to implicate Gatzke directly, the case to be made was largely circumstantial—and the circumstances pointed at him. He had insisted on adding the gun he had seen to the report he had made. He had described it in detail, which was as good as admitting it had been in his hands; and now that Gatzke had gotten rid of the actual gun, there was nothing to link him with any of it.

Gatzke pushed forward his shoulders in a genial shrug.

"And if you shot Nickel," he went on rather smugly, obviously amused, "no telling what else a jury will flip for. What *were* you doing so far downriver?"

Skinny did not know what to say to that because he was seeing events as they might be presented, wondering how believable it was that Ruth and he had just been out looking for driftwood.

Ishanti came around the bridge.

Skinny put Dwayne down, watching Ishanti now, not

wanting him to go after Gatzke; Ishanti knelt down by Dwayne then stood up again, holding his hand.

"Where you going with the boy?" Ishanti asked, quiet menace in his tone.

Before Gatzke could reply, Dwayne said, "I seen him before," and pointed his finger. "Seen him with my daddy."

"Yeah?" Ishanti said absently.

Dwayne nodded.

Skinny did not say anything because he knew that, since Gatzke had been working a case, placing him with Evans Charles didn't prove a thing.

"Seen him on my daddy's boat. Brought a big box of those guns."

Skinny dropped to one knee, looking at Dwayne now, listening carefully.

"A big wood box, took both of them to carry. I on the shore, in the grass, doing my business. Seen them."

"Nobody's going to believe that little monkey," Gatzke protested, momentarily forgetful of Ishanti.

Ishanti shifted his weight but stayed where he was.

"They didn't see you?" Skinny asked, catching a glimpse of Ruth and Mike Theriot near the bridge.

Dwayne shook his head no.

"Seen me later, when I finish."

Skinny looked hard at Don Gatzke, understanding it now, feeling contempt and disgust rise up in his throat. But he knew that he had him. There *was* a witness.

"And for that you were going to kill him. Because you didn't know. You didn't know *what* he had seen."

Gatzke looked from Ishanti to Skinny then back to Ishanti. Momentarily, he glanced over his shoulder at the bank of the river that was rapidly approaching.

"Better safe than sorry," he said to Skinny. "That's my

motto." He gave Ishanti a pained, sour smile, then without warning turned and dove into the river, going into the dirty brown water headfirst.

Ishanti stepped forward, looked around briefly, then deliberately replaced the cable across the gate.

"Man overboard," he said, but not very loudly.

42

From the ferry landing on the west bank of the river the view of New Orleans was spectacular. The two parallel bridges, the central business district, the French Quarter, even the Faubourg Marigny, were all clearly visible, a panorama. For almost two hours, the coast guard had been searching the river for Don Gatzke; New Orleans police were swarming up and down the levee and the batture. Skinny did not join in the search because he did not really care whether or not Gatzke was found: if he was he'd go to jail and if he wasn't he'd have to stay on the run—if he had drowned, so much the better. In any event, he was out of his life. So Skinny just watched all the activity, remaining very quiet for him, leaning on the rail on the pedestrian bridge to the ferry in a place that offered a particularly fine view, surprised somewhat when Ishanti came up beside him.

Ishanti assumed the same position Skinny was in, forearms on the upper rail, one foot on the lower, face into the bright sun and the breeze.

"I taking the boy home now," he said. "The police

through asking us questions. Ruth going to give us a ride to my car."

Skinny nodded.

"She wonder about me, about how I'll do by the boy. I told her, look in when she want. See how he doing."

Skinny nodded again.

"She say, the boy filled with anger, been through too much, need care."

Skinny looked over and saw that Ishanti was looking down at the river. He sensed that he wanted to say something else but could not find the words.

"The boy told me some things," he began. "He don't really know what he saying."

Skinny knew then what it was Ishanti was actually doing, making both a probe and a plea; and he knew then for certain what he had previously only suspected: that Dwayne was the other shooter, on the side opposite Gatzke when Nickel had been shot.

"Tell Henry not to tell anyone that Dwayne had a gun. Make sure he keeps his mouth shut."

For a long moment Ishanti's eyes locked on his.

"I take care of Henry," he said.

"That's for Dwayne," Skinny added. "I still owe you."

A slight smile touched Ishanti's lips.

"I think of something," he said.

"I'll just bet you will," Skinny replied.

Ishanti stood up straight, away from the rail. He seemed about to say something else then to decide against it. When he turned and went down the walkway, Skinny walked behind him, going down to the parking lot to see Ruth.

At Ishanti's approach, Dwayne got out of the front seat of the car and got back in in the back; but Ruth wasn't in the car.

"I'll go find her," Skinny said to Ishanti, "and tell her you're ready to go."

Ishanti got into the back of the car with Dwayne as Skinny turned and walked up the levee. Not far away he saw Ruth, down by the water, obviously taking some time for herself. For a few moments he just watched her.

Ruth had grown tired of answering questions, impatient with the search's slow progress; so when Dwayne had wanted to wait in the car for Ishanti, she had wandered away, finding herself drawn to the river. Near a single small tree, there was a deposit of sand, a small, temporary peninsula that extended a few feet out into the water. Viewed from that spit, the river seemed enormous, enormous and, though she knew better, very tranquil.

Considering the events of the last week, Ruth was surprised at how intact she felt. She knew she was only beginning to feel the relief, the release from tension. She knew she had a lot to sort out. When she saw Skinny approach, she stayed where she was and let him come up beside her. When he got near, he bent down and picked up a piece of driftwood about as long as and not much bigger around than a cane.

"Ishanti and Dwayne are ready to go," he said. "Ishanti said you're giving them a ride to his car."

Ruth acknowledged that she was, then held out her hand to take the piece of driftwood Skinny had found.

"What are you going to do?" she asked. She examined the piece of driftwood, admiring its soft, sculpted shape and its pale gray color, the whorls and lines in the exposed grain.

"I'll stick around for a while," Skinny replied. "I'll call you if anything happens."

"What about your truck?"

"Theriot had it towed. He'll give me a ride to the garage when it's fixed."

Ruth started to hand back the piece of driftwood, but Skinny waved in a way that indicated he didn't want it. She bent down to wash it off, deciding to keep it, using that as an excuse not to say anything else—there wasn't too much for Skinny and her *to* say really. There was an awkwardness between them they both felt, a distance they both knew would take some time to define.

A marked police car drove down the top of the levee. The policeman driving waved as he passed.

If Ruth had a particular regret it was that she had not been there when Skinny really needed her, which was, to her, more than a bit of a surprise because for so long— in many ways for her whole life—she had been waiting for just such a time, waiting and making preparation to accommodate a man and possibly a child. Yet within her doubts, within her failure to support him unquestioningly, what she had learned was that she wanted to be herself first, a fixed, solid person, without apology or confusion— then to make those decisions.

Wet, the piece of driftwood changed color, from pale gray to dark brown.

And the fact was, she was doing pretty well by it, if she had to say so herself. Her life was full just as she lived it, filled with possibility and potential and even some satisfaction.

"I'll go tell Ishanti and Dwayne you're on your way," Skinny said, obviously ready to go.

Ruth started to stand up to go with him, but she saw a piece of clay stuck to the driftwood. She decided to wash it again. For a few minutes, Ishanti and Dwayne and Skinny could just wait on her.